PEBBLEHOOF

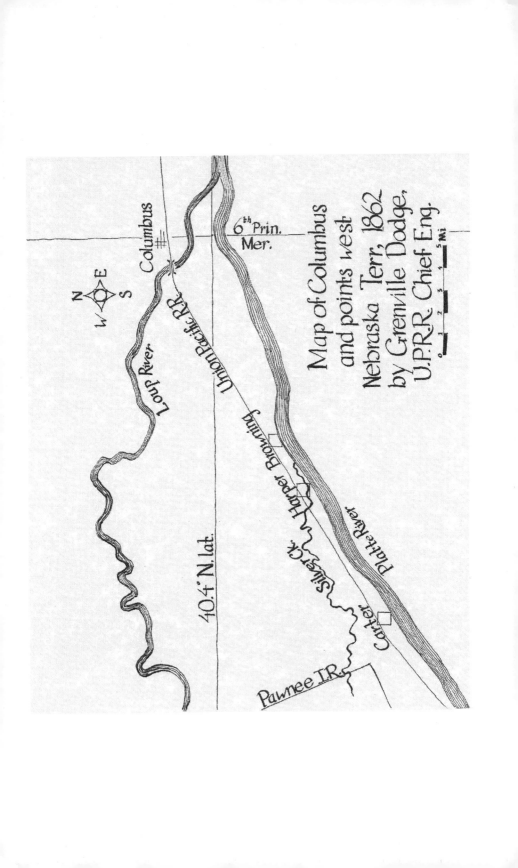

Map of Columbus
and points west
Nebraska Terr, 1862
by Grenville Dodge,
U.P.R.R. Chief Eng.

6ᵗʰ Prin.
Mer.

Columbus

N
W E
S

Loup River

Union Pacific R.R.

40.4° N. lat.

Browning

Harper

Silver Ck.

Carter

Platte River

Pawnee I.R.

0 1 2 3 4 5 Mi

PEBBLEHOOF
Jason Black

ELDER ROAD BOOKS
BELLEVUE, WA

ISBN 978-0-9856606-1-1

Book Design by Nathan Everett
ElderRoad@comcast.net

FOR MAIA

Anike –
Read like the wind!

[signature]

الساخد -
اكومه الله حامد نسطها!

CHAPTER 1

"**M**AMA, MUST I?" Maria Browning asked.

Laisa held out a shallow wicker basket and an iron hand-trowel. "Ach. All winter you complain you may not go out. Now spring is come und you want to stay in? Off with you!"

Maria took the basket and tucked the trowel reluctantly into the front pocket of her dress. "But it's so cold outside." She looked at her sister Klarina, playing with her rag doll by the warm cast-iron stove. "Can't Klarina do it?"

"Klarina has her own chores. She must scoop the ashes and sweep," said Laisa.

"But Mama—"

"Maria!" Her father's bark brought her up short. Bram's brow was furrowed, and the tight line of his mouth told her all she needed to know.

"Yes, Papa. I'm going."

Maria wrapped a shawl tightly around her shoulders.

Laisa asked, "You remember what it looks like?"

"I remember."

"Gut. And also sagewort, if you can find any."

"Yes, Mama."

Maria hopped up the two steps to the door of the Brownings' sod dugout cabin, and stepped into the bright April morning. She took care to close the door quickly.

Beyond the small, mowed clearing around the soddie, the wide prairie of the Nebraska Territory stretched out before her. The sweeping grasslands reached from horizon to horizon, interrupted only by the family's small stable and outhouse. Chicago, with its bustling streets, its tall wood-frame buildings set almost shoulder to shoulder, seemed like a whole other world now.

Maria held up a hand to shield her eyes against the morning glare. Somewhere out there, she had to find a stand of purple coneflower. *Back home,* she thought, *I could have just gone 'round to the corner apothecary.*

She pulled her shawl tighter and walked out into the tall grass. The brittle brown stalks of last year brushed against her hands, while the new green grass coated her shoes with a slick of dew.

The purple coneflower plants, which her mother wanted for their roots, were not yet in blossom, and would not be easy to find. Later, when their lovely flowers shot up high over the prairie grass, the chore would be simple. But now, as Maria discovered, it was not. She was a long way from the house and chilled, her fingers stiff with cold and her shoes soaked through, before she found a patch of plants whose leaves she recognized.

She nestled down, sheltering amid tall grasses from the light morning breeze. She began to dig. The plants did not give up their long, tough taproots easily.

Maria had claimed only one root from the soil when she heard it. A noise, low and rumbling. *Thunder*, she thought. She glanced at the sky to look for clouds, before realizing that the sound had not died away like thunder. It kept on, and was louder. She stood full up, and ran a few quick steps to the top of a rise. She looked back the way she had come, but saw nothing.

She spun the other way and saw them. Horses. A herd of wild horses, galloping across the prairie. Headed straight for her.

Maria had never had much love of horses. In Chicago, horses were huge beasts that clattered down the streets with wagons and carriages in tow, scattering people out of their way.

The herd bore down on her, wide across the landscape. They swarmed forward, faster than a bird in flight. She looked left and right. There was no chance of running out of their path.

She froze, rigid as ice, her eyes clenched shut and knuckles white around the handle of the trowel. *God preserve me,* she prayed, as the front line of pounding hooves reached her.

The ground shook. The noise was impossibly loud, deeper than thunder, but mixed with whinnies and nickers. Puffs of hot breath blew across her. Bits of flying earth peppered her face and she felt the occasional lash of a tail. She choked on dust and the smell of sweat.

But none of them touched her.

As quickly as they had come, they were past. The sound died away. Maria dared open her eyes. When the dust settled, the land around her was changed. Everything in the herd's path was trampled into the dirt, except for a small oval of grass centered exactly on her. She was the rock in the river, parting the herd around her like water.

Maria said a quick prayer of thanks and went down the gentle slope again to find her basket. It, too, was pounded to splinters and the patch of coneflowers reduced to earth.

Maria knelt down, fingering the bits of broken wicker, wondering how she would explain it to her mother.

Maria fought back a lump growing in her throat. *It's not fair!* In the solitude of the prairie, she dared to yell, to shout out loud what she had never dared say at home. "Why did we even come? I hate it here! Chicago was..."

She stopped. *I had friends in Chicago.* She remembered Angela and Hattie from the tenement building, who she had embroidered with and played dolls with. Friends she hadn't seen in almost a year. Friends who had not been there to celebrate her tenth birthday, just a week before.

But moping wouldn't get her chore done, and she could still find those roots down under the trampled soil. She set to digging again, and was deep in a tussle with a stubborn root when a sharp-edged shadow slid over her from behind. *Papa?* she wondered.

She turned to look, and met the enormous face of a dark brown stallion, just inches from her own. Its forehead was marked with a long white blaze that came nearly down to its nose. Its head was turned just to look at her with one eye.

Maria let out a short, sharp cry and scrambled backwards away from it. The horse did not startle, but only blinked its long, dusty eyelashes at her. It held its right front hoof just off the ground almost as if to shake hands.

The horse took a hesitant step forward, then picked the same hoof up again. It looked at her with its other eye. It took one more step, in the same ginger fashion.

"Oh, you're hurt." Maria said it out loud, not pausing to wonder whether it made any sense to talk to a horse. "Poor boy." For as little as Maria cared about horses, she knew enough to tell a stallion from a mare.

The horse took another awkward step towards her, putting so little weight on the one hoof that the step was almost a hop. He snuffled. His warm breath made Maria's hair move. The horse's calm demeanor, and Maria's curiosity, overcame her fear.

She stood slowly and approached his right side. Her head felt light, being so close to such a powerful animal. She could feel his heat radiating to her through the cold morning air. "You won't hurt me none, will you?"

The horse blinked again and swished his tail. She knelt down. "Let me see your foot now. Sorry, I mean your hoof." She reached out. The horse flinched slightly when she touched him, but stayed where he was.

She turned the hoof up to look at the bottom, and discovered a smooth stone wedged into a groove. "Oh! That must hurt, you poor thing." She looked up at him. His head was turned to watch her as best it could.

"This must have just happened, didn't it? Else your herd would have left you far behind by now. You just keep still, and I'll try to take it out."

She supported the hoof with one hand, and reached for the stone with the other. The horse flinched again when she touched it. "Easy now."

She waited for him to settle, then tried again. She pulled at the stone, but her fingers slipped off. It was small, no more than a pebble, and wedged tightly. Her fingers couldn't quite grip it. She tried a second time, then a third, but with no luck.

"Boy, it's really stuck." She thought what she might do. *The trowel!* Of course. "You wait right here," she said, and fetched the trowel from where it lay on the ground.

She settled herself in place once more and positioned the tip of the trowel where it seemed most advantageous. *Best do it quick.* "All right, boy. Here we go."

She thrust the handle of the trowel downwards in one quick motion, levering it against the hard edge of the horse's hoof.

The pebble popped out and flew off into the dirt. The horse flinched and whinnied, stumbling a step or two away from her.

Maria scrambled backwards again, letting the trowel fall to the ground. "Easy, easy!"

The horse shook his head, rippling his mane side to side. He carefully set the hoof down and took a trial step. Then another, more confidently. And another. He walked slowly over to her and whinnied softly.

He nuzzled her with his huge nose. Maria stood still, not at all sure how to respond. "You're welcome," she said. "You're all right now. You just had a little pebble in your hoof." She dared to reach up and pet him on his white blaze.

The horse blinked at her once more, then trotted away to follow the herd.

Maria stood, amazed as much by what she had done as what had happened. She watched as the horse sped from a trot to a full gallop, then vanished into the prairie.

CHAPTER 2

MARIA DUG UNTIL the sun was high in the sky, her stomach was rumbling, and her pile of roots was enough to fill her dress pockets and her hands. She hoped it would be enough to counter her mother's ire about the lost basket. And she hoped not to catch cold from being out all morning. She did not look forward to a dose of the bitter medicine her mother brewed from these roots. Coneflower tea was Laisa's preferred cure-all, and the family had run their stock out over the long winter.

When she came near enough to the family's low, sod cabin, she saw an unfamiliar horse tied to the paddock fence outside. *A visitor?* Maria couldn't even remember the last time anyone had been by. Before Christmas, certainly. She hurried her steps.

Inside, she found her father sitting by the wood stove, talking with a man she recognized. The Reverend Tinney. He had visited them every so often the previous year, while Papa was cutting sod, digging out for the house, and setting up the homestead.

Everyone turned to look at her as she came in. The reverend

smiled at her. "Why, Maria. I do believe you've grown a full head since last autumn." He spared a glance at Laisa. "Must be your mother's good German cooking."

Maria gave what curtsey she could, with her hands and dress stuffed full of roots. "Good day to you, Reverend."

Bram, however, paid her scant attention. "Go on, Reverend. What were you saying about the railroad?"

"Oh, sir, it is a sure thing now and indeed a blessing for the whole Platte River valley."

Maria listened in while she set to washing the roots in a wooden bucket and hanging them to dry. Laisa stood at the table, mixing up something in a bowl. Laisa leaned towards Maria, and mouthed the word *basket*.

Maria bit her lip and shrugged. Her mother glared briefly. Maria knew her scolding would wait until the reverend had gone.

Reverend Tinney continued. "The route of the great Trans-Continental railroad has been determined to come through Columbus, and from there, directly along the Platte for some ways."

"Is this true?" There was no mistaking the excitement in Bram's voice. "A railroad man came through last year, in the fall, to—what is the word? He looked at the land to see if it is gut."

"To survey, you mean?"

"Ja, he make a survey. Und now it is certain the railroad will come here?"

"Quite certain. I came from Columbus this very morning, where the Union Pacific company has begun work on a depot. Yes, think of it, Mr. Browning," the reverend went on, "a great highway of goods, stretching from coast to coast, passing practically outside your door. Soon, Columbus will be a booming town, to the benefit of every homesteader for miles around."

"Oh, Laisa," Bram said, a smile huge on his face, "do you hear?"

Laisa looked up from her work and beamed at her husband.

A railroad, here? It sounded exciting, but Maria was puzzled as to how it would benefit them. She longed to ask, but knew she must not interrupt.

Reverend Tinney said, "Pray with me, sir. Let us praise the Lord, for bringing us this great fortune."

Bram held up a hand. "I thank you for this wonderful news, Reverend, but you may thank Gott in your way und I shall thank him in mine."

"Oh, I don't mean to presume, Mr. Browning. There is much wisdom in the Lutheran faith. It is only my hope to show you what Baptist tradition offers as well."

A nervous feeling rose in Maria's belly. Nice as it was to have a visitor, Reverend Tinney's visits always ended this way. The reverend clutched his small black Bible to his chest, closed his eyes, and mumbled a quiet prayer. Bram did not. He would say his thanks at grace around the supper table.

Tinney finished his prayer and shook Bram's hand. "Until next time, Mr. Browning. Thank you for your congenial hospitality. I am pleased to bring you such good news. However, I must be off. I do believe my horse has a loose shoe. I must pay a visit on your neighbor Mr. Harper. You're lucky to have a good horseman like him so nearby."

"Ja. Auf Wiedersehen, Reverend."

Bram saw the man out. When the door was closed, he sprang lightly over to the table, swooped up Laisa in his arms, and danced her around the little room.

"Bram!" Laisa laughed.

"Did you hear, my darling? Did you hear? Years we can save. Years! Mein Gott, I must plant my orchard now. So soon, I know, but Columbus will need a printer, ja?"

"Ja, Bram. Sehr gut."

Bram held Laisa in a tight embrace. When he let her go, Maria dared ask, "Papa. What's it all about?" As long as everyone was so happy, perhaps her mother would forget about the basket.

He gave her a broad smile. "Oh, mein Schatzie, it is wonderful. So many workers in Columbus, they need to eat. We will have no trouble to sell everything we grow this year, und next year. We will make so much money in two years, maybe, as I had thought in five. Columbus will grow, with a railroad depot. The town, she will need a printer to make newspaper und handbills. That will be us, Maria."

"But, why must you plant an orchard? What does fruit have to do with it?"

Bram laughed. "Not fruit. Walnuts. To press for the oil. Is good for making ink." Bram brought his hands together in a single, sharp clap. "But, good news will not milk the cow." He gathered up the milking buckets and stepped outside.

A moment passed. Klarina, who had been playing quietly on the bed with some beads on a string, asked, "Maria, what happened to your basket?"

Maria shot Klarina a dirty look.

"Ja," Laisa asked. "Where is it?"

Maria's voice caught in her throat. The story of the wild herd stampeding all around her, the terror and excitement of it, the words pressed against her teeth and lips but would not come out. It hadn't been her fault at all, what happened, but she knew how it would sound if she said it. It would sound like a lie, and that would be worse.

"I—I just lost it. That's all."

Laisa folded her arms and looked sternly at her daughter. "Maria, how could you? My good wicker basket."

Maria hung her head, looking down at the smudges of dirt on her dress.

"Well. What is done is done," Laisa said. "Anyhow, it is time I teach you girls how to weave baskets yourselves."

She handed Maria a short, sharp knife. "Go down to the river and cut as much willow as you can carry. Thin, new switches, the size of your small finger. Hurry now."

Maria ran out.

Before she had left the yard, her mother called after her. "Und don't lose the knife!"

CHAPTER 3

MARIA BROUGHT HOME a thick bundle of willow switches. Laisa told her to put them in a barrel full of water, so they would stay soft and pliable, and set her the task of stripping them of their bark.

The bark, brownish green on the outside but bright, spring green on the inside, would not be thrown out. Maria peeled the bark in long strips, which she tied in bunches so they could be hung up to dry. Laisa would use them to brew the tea Bram drank, morning and night, to ease the pain in his back.

When Bram came in after finishing the day's chores, he kissed Maria on the top of her head. "Oh, fresh willow. Thank you for that, my good girl." He stoked up the wood stove while Laisa prepared supper, and sat with his back towards the hot iron.

The next morning, Laisa sat Maria and Klarina on the edge of their bed. "Now watch me," she instructed, as she gathered a handful of the willow. The girls watched as Laisa split each willow switch at its thick end, carefully cutting down its length to produce two even halves. She laid these in pairs across her hand, and showed the girls how to weave a third split-switch over and under, spiraling out from the center.

Laisa's fingers flew, gathering speed as she went, coiling the third switch around and around to form a small circle. As the circle grew, she added new spokes, and in no time had formed the soft willow into a flat circle the size of a dinner plate. The ends of the spokes stuck out from the circle. *Like a big willow spider*, Maria thought.

"Mama, where did you learn that?" Klarina asked.

"When I was a small girl, just like you. My mama taught me. It is what my family did, back in Germany. Before your papa and I came to America."

"I didn't know that," Maria said.

"Ja. Well, in the city there was no willow. We must buy such things. Here, we can do for ourselves."

Indeed, Maria had never seen a willow bush until the first time her family had forded a small river, on their journey west the previous year.

"Now," Laisa said. "You girls try. Make more, just like this. This is the bottom of the basket. Later, I show you how to make the sides. But now you weave while I start the bread."

She left the willow spider out for the girls to look at. Maria quickly discovered her mother had made a tricky job look simple. Her switches would not split so evenly, and she had a devil of a time keeping her spokes still while weaving the spiral.

Her first spider, she reckoned, looked like their farm horse Poppy had stepped on it.

Maria wove willow all morning, as much helping Klarina as working on her own. As she worked, her thoughts drifted back to the horse with the pebble in his hoof. She wondered where the herd was now, and if she'd ever see them again. He was a big horse, and somewhat frightful, but Maria had felt a gentleness in him too. She was glad she had helped him.

A FEW DAYS later, Papa hurried through his daily chores. He conscripted Maria to help finish them early so he could rush off to Columbus. "I must order a book on how to make an orchard," he said.

"I thought you already knew all that, Papa," Maria asked, as they stacked newly-chopped firewood.

"How to print, ja. How to set type und make the ink. I learn this in my father's shop, and a little more in Chicago. But always the oil was bought. Here, I must make it myself, und for that, I must learn how to grow my own trees."

When the wood was stacked, Bram made ready for the trip. He put half a loaf of Laisa's fresh bread and a wedge of cheese in a small sack. He slung a bedroll on his back, took his rifle down from its pegs on the wall, and set out for Columbus. He would sleep there that night, conduct his business in the morning, and return home by dinner the next day.

With the chores done so early, Maria found herself with the luxury of a day to herself. She had yet to shake the cramped, crowded feeling left over from being stuck in the soddie all winter with her family, and asked her mother if she might walk in the prairie.

"Ja. Watch out for snakes, und be home for supper."

"Yes, Mama."

Maria walked with no particular destination in mind. It was so quiet and still, out in the open. Nothing like back home in Chicago, where there was always something to listen to. People talking in the street, babies crying somewhere in the tenement. Always in Chicago, there was the sound of life happening. *But not out here,* she thought. On the prairie, there was little more than the sound of wind in the grass and her own footsteps to keep her company.

Without guidance, her feet carried her back towards where the herd had found her. It was not difficult to find the herd's trail of pounded earth, now showing a thin layer of fresh green shoots poking through the soil.

The trail ran roughly northeast, somewhat towards the town of Columbus. Maria wondered briefly if Papa had ever seen the herd on days when he was out hunting. If he had, he never said so.

She followed the trail for a while, glad to stretch her legs. Quiet it might be, but Maria allowed that it was at least good to be outside now that spring had come. Chicago didn't have anything like the prairie's endless, wide open space to walk in.

The prairie, which looked so flat from the family's homestead, was in truth a sea of gentle waves. Rolling undulations in the grass. She imagined herself a ship, sailing the grassy sea. She ran, laughing, down the backsides of the waves, following the herd's trail.

Late in the afternoon, she spied them. Perhaps another half mile away, down in a shallow depression. Their heads were all down, grazing on the new spring grasses. Maria strained her eyes, wondering if her horse was amid them somewhere, hoping he had made his way back to the herd. *Pebblehoof,* she thought. *That's a good name. Are you out there, Pebblehoof?*

She had a mind to cross that half mile and look for him. But the sun was sinking low. Night was coming, and if she wasn't home by suppertime she would be in a world of trouble. Maria left the herd and headed back to the homestead. As she went, she promised herself she would find him another time. *And the next time, I'll get closer.*

CHAPTER 4

BRAM WAS BACK from Columbus. Maria was helping measure out spots for walnut trees when a man on horseback appeared in the distance.

"Papa, look," Maria said, pointing at the approaching stranger.

Bram looked, and raised his hand to wave. The stranger waved back.

"Who is it?" she asked.

"I do not know. We will go to the house and meet him there. Hurry now."

Bram walked in brisk strides back to the cabin. Maria had to run to keep up with him. Bram took down his rifle and sent Maria inside.

"Don't worry, Schatzie. I am only being careful."

Maria and Laisa watched from the doorway as the stranger approached. Klarina peeked out from behind her mother's skirts. Bram stood calmly, with the rifle slung over the crook of one arm. Not aimed, but ready.

The stranger rode slowly. When he reached the stable, he called out, "Hallo!" From the darkness inside the house, Maria squinted out at the man. He seemed friendly enough, and she could not see any gun.

The man dismounted next to the paddock. "May I tie up here, sir?" he asked.

Bram nodded. He lowered the rifle a notch, but did not put it away. "Maria," he called back to the house, "bring water."

Maria fetched the wooden water bucket from inside the house and the tin dipper. She carried it to the man.

"Thank you, miss," he said.

She waited while he drank. He was dressed in leather boots, pants of store-bought denim, and a heavy flannel shirt. The broad brim of a well-worn hat shaded his face.

"Ah," he sighed, as he handed back the bucket and the dipper. "That surely does ease a dusty throat."

Maria scampered back to her father's side. The man strode up, his hand outstretched.

"My name's Silas Seymour. I thank you for the water. What might I call you, sir?"

Bram introduced himself and asked, "Does your horse need water?"

"Thank you, no. I'll ride her down to the river." Mr. Seymour put his hands on his hips and surveyed the homestead. "Nice piece of land you have here, Mr. Browning."

"Ja. Are you scouting for a homestead? There is good land upriver. Not far."

"Oh, no sir. Not me. I'm with the railroad. I'm out visiting all the homesteads on this stretch of the Platte."

Bram's face lit up. He handed the rifle to Maria. "Put this away, Schatzie." To Mr. Seymour he said, "Ja, such wonderful news that the railroad will be in Columbus. But what brings you out here?"

Maria returned the rifle to its pegs inside, and took up her position in the doorway again.

"I'm making a survey of the line, sir."

Bram cocked his head to one side. "But, did not someone already do this? A man came through last year, in the fall."

Silas Seymour nodded. "Indeed so. That would be Mr. Dodge, the Union Pacific's chief engineer. He made the initial survey. The time has come to make a more careful survey, to establish the final lay of the line."

"I do not understand. Mr. Dodge seemed very final. He agreed to have five acres from one corner of my quarter-section as..." Bram paused. "I do not remember the English for it. Eine Grunddienstbarkeit. I have it on a paper inside."

"An easement?" Mr. Seymour asked.

"Ja! That is it. For five acres, at ten dollars to the acre. To be paid when the railroad is built. He put in markers for it also."

"Did he now? I will take a look at them. But you must understand, Mr. Browning. That was only the initial survey. The final line is bound to be different."

"But I have it on a document. Mr. Dodge signed it."

"But no money changed hands, is that correct?"

Bram crossed his arms. "Nein. Not yet."

"Then nothing is binding, Mr. Browning. But calm yourself. There is no reason for concern before I have even done my work."

"Very well. Where do you think will it be, then?"

Seymour pointed east towards Columbus, and swooped his hand indicating a path westward. "Right here along the Platte River, sir. A steam engine needs water, you know."

Bram's back stiffened, his head rising up a notch. "How close by the river? My land runs down to bank."

"Well, clearly not at the water's very edge, Mr. Browning. Some distance back, of course."

"What distance?" Maria could not see her father's face, the way he was standing, but his voice betrayed the hard furrow in his brow.

"I don't yet know. That's why I must take a survey." Mr. Seymour's posture also stiffened. "You do want the railroad to come through, do you not?"

"Of course. But this is my land. It is well marked. Come, I will show you my marker posts."

Mr. Seymour held up a hand. "No need, sir. I saw your northeast post as I rode in. I can find them."

"Will you promise your railroad will not cross my land?"

Mr. Seymour looked down at his boots. "I promise you, Mr. Browning, that the Union Pacific Railroad company will take homesteaders into account when making its plans. Now, if you are amenable, I do need to measure the distance from the river to your markers—"

Bram interrupted. "Und Mr. Dodge's markers."

"Yes, and Mr. Dodge's markers. Don't trouble yourself on my account. I'll attend to my business and be on my way."

"Ja. You do that."

Bram stood rigid while Mr. Seymour untied his mare and led her back towards Bram's northeast marker post. Laisa and the girls came out to join him once the man was away.

"All is well, Bram?" Laisa asked.

Bram was silent for a long moment. "Ja. I suppose so." Maria expected her father to lead her back out to measure off the rest of the orchard, but Bram did not move. The Brownings watched together as Mr. Seymour withdrew the necessary equipment from his saddle bags, walked to the marker posts, and took his measurements.

CHAPTER 5

PEBBLEHOOF WAS NEVER far from Maria's mind. She thought about him often, wondering if his hoof was well, and whether she would ever find him again. On a Thursday, the sun rose to a clear day. *Today*, Maria thought. She raced through her chores, airing out the bedclothes and cleaning the breakfast dishes.

As she worked, she thought. Laisa was tending the garden outside, and Maria knew she would need a plan. Something that would get her away from the house.

When her chores were done, she said "Stay here, Klarina. I'm going out."

"I want to go too," Klarina said. She jumped up, letting her rag doll fall to the floor.

"You can't, Klarie," said Maria. "You haven't done your work yet."

"Do I have to?" Klarina's shoulders slumped down.

Maria took up the basket she had completed, under her mother's guidance, to replace the one that was lost. It wasn't nearly so pretty or tightly woven as the one her mother made, but she was proud of it just the same. "Yes you have to, and be glad Mama isn't in to hear you complain! Now clean out the ashes, and sweep the floor. Then ask Mama if you can go out."

Klarina grumbled, but picked up the broom.

"No, silly," Maria said. "Scoop the ashes first, then sweep."

"But the bucket's almost full," Klarina said.

Maria glanced at the ash bucket, made from an old barrel that didn't quite hold water anymore. It was about half full. "There's plenty of room. Now settle down. Moaning never got any work done."

Maria looked through her mother's earthenware jars of herbs, until she found one that was almost empty. She sniffed it. *Just the thing*, she thought.

Klarina had the iron scoop in hand and door to the cold wood stove open as Maria stepped outside. She strolled over to the garden, where Laisa knelt in the soft soil, planting cabbage seedlings she had started indoors.

"What is it, Schatzie?"

"I finished my chores. Can I go out and look for sagewort? Your jar is almost empty."

"Is it? What a good girl you are."

"I can go?"

"Ja, danke. You know how it looks?"

Maria nodded. "I remember."

MARIA RAN EXCITEDLY, her basket dangling from one hand. It was good to stretch her legs. She ran until she was winded, slowed to walk, and stopped.

She had no idea where the herd might be. It had been days since she had seen the herd in the distance. They could have walked or galloped anywhere. She put the midday sun at her back and went north, away from the river. The land sloped gently upward in that direction, taking her higher to where she hoped she might see farther.

She saw a clump of sagewort, but passed it by. If she saw the herd, she wanted to be able to run, but couldn't do that with a basket of herbs. She would find more on her way home.

The sun warmed her as she walked through the tall, thick grass. Flocks of light brown birds rose up as she passed. The tiny birds settled again some distance away, holding sideways onto the tall brown stalks of last year's growth. Once, the shadow of a hawk flickered over her, on the lookout for field mice or perhaps a rabbit. She wondered where the hawks kept their nests.

After what felt like a great deal of walking, Maria stopped to look back. She was rewarded by a wide-open view of the prairie, sloping down behind her the way she had come. The soddie and the stable were just two small, dark bumps in the landscape, far away. She traced the Platte River upstream, trying to find Mr. Harper's house even though she knew it was too distant to see.

But in the direction of Mr. Harper's house, she saw a dusky patch on the land. Not a house. Not a stand of trees. Horses. *There they are!*

They were a long ways off. More than a mile. Maybe two. Maria set off at a run, the tiredness in her legs forgotten.

Running through the tall grass was difficult, but after a time she encountered the wagon trail, and running was easier. It was the same trail her family had followed the previous year, worn into the land by homesteaders settling the Platte River valley and points farther west all the way to the Oregon Territory. She was glad her father had not wanted to go so far as that.

But Maria did not care where the trail stopped. She only cared that this line through the prairie, worn into the land by so many wagons, now led her towards the herd. Towards Pebblehoof.

The dark mass of horses, like the shadow of a thundercloud, dipped in and out of sight as Maria bobbed up and down the prairie's rolling landscape.

She stopped only once, briefly, to quench her thirst at a small stream. And when she thought she could run no more, when the noon sun was high and her shadow reduced to a small spot beneath her, she reached them.

She stopped, a few hundred feet away. The basket fell to the ground as Maria stooped over. She breathed hard, gripping her knees for support, as she watched them.

The herd ambled slowly through the grass. Black, brown, dappled, and dun. Mares and stallions. Colts and foals. Every kind of horse Maria could ever imagine drifted along, their heads down, feeding on the sweet spring grass. The breeze shifted towards her, almost overpowering her with the smell of them.

When she caught her breath, she stood upright to search.

"Pebblehoof!" she called out. "It's me. You remember, I helped you before."

A few horses lifted their heads to look at her. Some shied away, but most seemed to consider her harmless and bent down again to continue eating.

None of them had the white blaze she was looking for.

But the herd was large, so many she couldn't possibly count them. *He must be in there somewhere.* She called to him again, darting her eyes every time a horse lifted its head, and walked closer.

Her heart pounded as she approached them. Their towering size made her feel so very, very tiny. She spoke in a low voice, "It's all right. I'm not going to hurt anybody. Just let me pass." She talked and talked, as much to reassure herself as them.

She reached them. So close, she couldn't help but stretch out her fingers to touch the flank of a golden-yellow mare. The mare nickered, and she jerked her arm back.

This close, the herd was a great wall of horses, their shoulders just higher than the top of her head. It was impossible to see anything. To find him, she might have to enter the herd. The thought of making her way between the massive, moving animals was terrifying.

But I could see from the front. She noticed that the herd had its heads all facing the same way, as they moved together across the prairie. She trotted off the trail, into the grass and ahead of them. She could see their heads much better this way, and decided to try calling once more.

"Pebblehoof!"

Several of them looked up at her. *There!* Near the outside edge of the herd, on the side that had been farthest from her before, she saw him. She ran to him, and a moment later was at his side.

"Here you are! I've been looking for you."

The horse gazed at her again with its huge black eyes.

"You remember me, don't you? Sure you do."

She reached out to stroke the glossy hair on his neck. He whinnied softly, and stopped walking, but put his head down to keep eating.

Maria crouched down beside him. "How's your hoof?" Pebblehoof nuzzled her, his huge head nearly tipping her backwards off her haunches.

She wanted to take a look at the bottom side of the hoof again, but that hoof was on the far side from her now, in with all the other horses, and she dared not.

But a thought did cross her mind. Something she just might dare try. *I'll bet I can ride him.*

She stood up and set a hand on his withers, just like she had seen her papa do so many times with Poppy. She felt Pebblehoof's flesh ripple under her hand, but he didn't bolt.

"Good boy, Pebblehoof. You don't mind if I call you that, do you?"

Pebblehoof took a small step forward to reach an uneaten tuft of green.

"That's right. I'm just going to get up on you, now. You don't mind? Big horse like you? Of course not."

But she had a problem. Pebblehoof had no saddle. Where Bram would reach his foot to a stirrup, there was nothing. She stood there, pondering what to do, while her hand rested on Pebblehoof's warm shoulder.

At last she said, "Well, if the Indians don't need saddles, I reckon I can get by. Keep still now."

Pebblehoof took another small step. Maria adjusted her position and worked her plan through in her mind. She hiked up her skirts so she could move her legs freely, almost blushing at how much she knew her parents would not approve. *Not very ladylike, but there's nobody out here to see me.*

Then, with a quick crouch and a jump, she flung herself upward. She stretched one arm across the horse's wide breadth and got her foot up on his haunches, draping herself awkwardly down Pebblehoof's side.

This time Pebblehoof did twitch, jumping forward a few quick steps. Maria lost her grip and flopped down onto the ground. Her cheek landed on a fresh, dark green horse dropping that had rolled a hand span away from a much larger pile.

She picked herself up, yanked up a handful of grass to wipe her face, and strode over to him again.

Pebblehoof moved away from her.

"Come on now," she said, in the same soft and low voice as before. "I only want to ride a bit. Won't hurt you none at all."

She matched his movements, stroking his flank, and presently he calmed down again.

"There's a good boy." She took her stance again, determined to jump higher. "Now let me on this time. Can't you lower down just a little?"

She remembered something her father had explained on the wagon ride out from Chicago. He had been teaching Laisa how to drive the wagon, in case the need arose. Maria had wanted to learn too, but knew he wouldn't let her. She was too little. He had said, "They will move away from the pressure of the reins. You do not need to pull hard."

Maria wondered if wild horses acted the same way. She put both hands on Pebblehoof's withers, and gently eased her weight downward. "Lower down, now. Come on. Be a good boy. I'm sorry I don't have anything to give you," for she knew you were supposed to give horses carrots to make them behave, "but you can do it anyhow, can't you?"

And to Maria's great amazement, Pebblehoof knelt down. He looked at her with one big eye, and knelt for her.

"Good boy!" Maria wasted no time. Climbing on was easy now. She swung her leg up high and slid onto Pebblehoof's back, surprised at the great width of him. He twisted and shook underneath her. She lay down on his back, her arms holding on to either side of him.

"Easy now, easy."

Without warning, Pebblehoof stood up again. It was like the earth itself thrusting her upwards. She held on for all she was worth, eyes clenched shut, as Pebblehoof took a few steps to catch up with the herd.

Laid down upon him, Maria felt the rhythmic motion of his walk. With her ear pressed to the base of his mane, she heard the deep, powerful beating of his heart. With her hands grasping his sides, she felt the movement of ribs, in and out with every breath.

She could think of nothing she had ever done in all her life that was as exciting as this.

She held on, eyes closed and lying down, just feeling the horse's strength and power. The smell of horse and dust filled her nose.

When she dared open her eyes, she saw that Pebblehoof had drifted inside the herd. She was surrounded on all sides by horses. But she did not panic. Pebblehoof had her. *He won't let me come to any harm.*

She sat up, giddy at being up so high, but kept her hands on his withers. For just an instant, as she found her balance on Pebblehoof's shifting back, she remembered she had left her basket behind. But she didn't care, not now. She could always go back for it.

The herd ambled along the prairie. Maria watched their movements, fascinated by how the horses would drift slowly to the outside of the herd. How they paused on the periphery to eat, moving only at a slow walk while the rest kept on, before rejoining again at the back after the herd had passed them.

She floated among them on Pebblehoof's broad back, out and back in again, as the horses made their peaceful dance across the prairie.

The land began to slope down. The herd was moving faster now, arcing around to her right, down towards the river. And then, Maria almost did panic. *Will they stop?* she wondered. What if they crossed the river? What if she fell in? And if they did cross it, how would she ever get back? The river was high with spring melt. She'd be swept clean away.

She almost jumped off right then, to take her chances on foot inside the herd. But she didn't. She held on, where she was safe, at least for the moment.

The herd moseyed down to the water, picking its way through the trees and stands of willow in the bottom land. The horses spread themselves wide along the banks, and Maria's fear eased. They did not try to cross the swift water, but only lowered their heads to drink.

Maria almost laughed with relief. *Of course they wouldn't try to cross now*, she thought. *They're smart enough to wait until the river comes down.*

Maria rode with the herd a long time—sometimes near the middle, sometimes on the edges, sometimes out at the very front of them all—as Pebblehoof moved this way and that among his brethren. She rode a long time, enjoying her view from so high. Like being on top of the world.

She could have ridden forever, except for two things. For one, it was late. The sun was dropping into the west, and her stomach was complaining that she had missed dinner. For the other, she had to pee.

The next time Pebblehoof made his way to the edge of the herd, Maria said "Whoa there, boy. I have to get off now. She pressed down again on his withers. "Kneel down for me. Come on."

It took a moment, but Pebblehoof obliged. Maria slid off to one side. "Good boy." Pebblehoof turned his head to nuzzle at her, and she found herself kissing the side of his nose.

"I'll find you again," she said. "I promise I will. Thanks for the ride."

Pebblehoof trotted back to the herd, leaving Maria on her own once again. But she was grateful for the solitude, since there was no outhouse anywhere nearby. She crouched down in the grass and relieved herself.

When she stood, her shadow stretched out long to the east, and she swallowed hard. *I'm late.* Her parents would be worried. There was no time to go back for the basket now, nor even to pick the sagewort she had promised.

She took a moment to look around, figuring the direction back to the homestead, and set out at a run.

CHAPTER 6

MARIA RAN AS though trying to catch her shadow, though it stayed forever just ahead of her. She wondered, as her feet beat out a steady rhythm, what she would tell her parents when she returned. *I'll say I was lost,* she thought.

That didn't explain the basket, but it might get her out of the worst of the trouble she was in, especially if she could get home quickly.

The low places of the rolling landscape were in shadow now. They swallowed her in darkness as she descended into the hollows, yielding her back to the fading light as she gained the crests. The sun lowered behind her until all was in shadow.

At last, she caught sight of a building in the twilight, its chimney just catching the last rays of sun. Maria's spirits rose, but only for a moment. There was a house and a stable, but the stable was on the wrong side of the house, and was much larger than the one Papa had built.

Mr. Harper's place. She slowed in disappointment. The warmth of the soddie, lantern light—and likely a sound thrashing—were still two full miles farther on.

Those and a warm supper. Already her stomach ached with emptiness and her head felt dizzy. She took a deep breath to press onward, but as she passed Mr. Harper's home, the door opened.

She saw the dark silhouette of her neighbor, framed in the orange glow of his doorway, the thin line of a rifle at his side. "Who's that?" he called. "I know you're there."

Maria wondered if she might better ask to spend the night. She did not like the idea of making her way home in the darkness, when prairie wolves could be about.

"It's Maria Browning, Mr. Harper," she called back.

He stepped outside. With one foot he blocked his dog from dashing out, then closed the door. "Land sakes, child," he hollered back at her. "Is all well? What brings you here so late?" He strode over to her, and was soon by her side.

Maria explained that she had not intended to come, but was only passing by. Heat flushed in her face, and she was glad of the concealing darkness.

"Well thank the Lord for that," Mr. Harper said. "I was afeared someone was ill or hurt."

Maria swallowed hard, embarrassed to ask what she was thinking. "I wonder, sir, may I sleep in your stable and continue on in the morning? I shouldn't like to make my way home in such darkness."

Mr. Harper pulled at his scraggly beard. After a moment he said, "No, miss. I don't reckon that'd be wise." Maria's heart sank. Then he continued, "No, I expect I'd best see you home now. Your mam and pap'll be out beating the bushes for you. Come along."

Maria thanked him as he led her to his own stable, where he saddled up a mare.

Maria asked, "How many horses have you, Mr. Harper?"

"Well, I've got Bessie here for ridin'," he said, patting the mare on her flank. "I've got Elias and Elijah for the farm. They're my work team. Then there's Bessie's colt, and I ain't settled on a name for him yet."

He led Bessie out, and with a smooth motion flung himself up into the saddle. He settled his feet in the stirrups and reached down to her. "Hop up now. You can ride behind me. Plenty of space on Bessie's rump."

Maria took his hand. He swung her up like she weighed no more than a sack of flour.

Mr. Harper clicked with his tongue, and Bessie set off.

"Aren't we going to bring a lantern?"

"No need," said Mr. Harper. "We're on the wagon trail, and Bessie knows the way."

Maria thought on how strange it was, for her to be up on a second horse in the same day, when she had never been on horseback at all before. She had, of course, ridden endless miles behind horses, in the wagon on the family's journey from Chicago, but had never sat up on one.

But the similarity ended there. Maria couldn't help but notice how different it was, sitting up high on Bessie in the dark, scarcely able to see the ground. On Pebblehoof, she had surveyed the whole world around her, free and mighty. On Bessie, the darkness and the empty space seemed to press in at her. She held tight to Mr. Harper's waist.

After a while, Mr. Harper said, "Miss Browning, there's something sets my mind to worry. I seen which way you come from. That's Pawnee land, not too far west from here."

Maria swallowed. "You mean Indians?" She had known they were around, somewhere, but had never seen any.

"Yes'm. 'Nother ten miles on, maybe fifteen. Uncle Sam give 'em a patch of land and a treaty. Now, mostly they keep to themselves. Still, could be dangerous down that way, all by yourself in the dark. So naturally I can't help but wonder just how you came to be outside my door this evening."

Maria almost told him she had gotten lost, then stopped herself and said nothing. *That won't work at all*, she thought. It might work for Mr. Harper, but if her parents thought she had truly lost her way on the prairie, they would never let her go out like that again. And then she'd never get to ride Pebblehoof anymore. At last she said, "I shouldn't like to say, sir. But I'll stay clear of the Pawnees."

"Fair enough. None of my business anyhow," he said. "That's between you and your folks, I reckon. Just you keep yourself safe out here."

"Yes, sir."

"But if you were in any trouble, I hope you would ask me for help. Neighbors got to watch out for one another out here. You in any trouble, miss?"

"No. Leastwise, not until I get home."

Mr. Harper chuckled. "Well, now, don't you worry overmuch. They'll be mad, I'm sure, but grown folks remember when they was chilluns too."

They said no more until at last Mr. Browning turned Bessie off the trail. He dismounted some ways from the house and helped Maria down. "Hallo, Brownings!" he hollered out. "It's Mr. Harper and your Maria."

The door was open before Mr. Harper had even finished talking. Maria saw Laisa's thick-set frame bolt out, lantern in hand. She ran across the yard and dropped to her knees in front of Maria, swooping her up into an embrace.

She squeezed Maria hard, then held her out at arm's length, a look of fire in her eyes, and slapped Maria across one cheek. "You wicked, wicked girl! You had me sick with worry. Gehst hinein!"

Maria knew she was really in trouble. Mama and Papa tried their best to speak English, but when they were angry the German came out. Maria did as she had been told and fetched herself inside. Behind her, she heard her mother inviting Mr. Harper in.

Her father glared at her when she came in, but even so it felt good to be back. "Sit," he ordered, and pointed towards the bed where Klarina was lying down, already in her nightclothes.

She sat, mute, while Bram and Laisa greeted Mr. Harper, offered him coffee, and thanked him over and over for bringing her home. "Bram was just about to go out himself to look," Laisa said.

"T'warn't any bother, Ma'am," he said. "And another time I would be pleased to stay for that coffee, but I left a pot of stew over the coals. I'd best fetch up home before that dog of mine eats up my supper."

He took his leave, but spared a quick wink at Maria on his way out.

No sooner had the door closed than the questions began. "Where have you been? What were you doing? We thought you must be dead!"

Maria was at a loss for words. She shouldn't lie, but she dared not say what she had really done, either. Riding a wild horse? They would never approve. If they learned about Pebblehoof, they would surely forbid her from ever going out again.

"Answer your mother, Maria," Bram said. "What were you doing out so late, and all the way to Mr. Harper's?"

Maria looked down at her shoes. "I—I just lost track of the time, that's all." That much was true, anyway. "I forgot to watch the sun."

"How did you come to be so far away?" Laisa went on. "And

what is that you have on your face?"

Maria darted her hand up to her cheek where, sure enough, she felt a dried flake of horse manure clinging there.

Laisa did not wait for an answer. "And where is your basket? You are gone all day and you do not even bring the sagewort? Shameful."

"It's on the trail somewhere," Maria said. "Out past Mr. Harper's. I'll go get it in the morning, I promise, and I'll bring it back full of sagewort. The best I can find." Maria could feel the tightness in her chest that told her tears were coming, but she pushed it back. She must not cry.

"Ach, never mind!" Laisa snatched up a rag from the wash basin and threw it at Maria. "Wash your face and get into bed. No supper for you tonight. Perhaps hunger will teach you a lesson."

Maria's stomach growled out loud in protest, but she dared not complain. "Yes, Mama."

She cleaned herself and changed into her nightdress. Klarina watched her, looking as if she were about to cry too. Maria longed to tell Klarina everything was all right, but she knew she had best not say anything else.

When her clothes were hung up and her shoes set at the foot of the bed, Bram said, "Come here, Maria."

Knowing what was coming, she went to where he sat by the cook stove. His tin cup of willow bark tea sat on top of the stove, just like always, keeping warm while he drank down the bitter stuff.

Bram turned her over his knee and paddled her bottom, harder than she could remember having ever been spanked. She held her lips in a tight line, and did not cry.

When it was over, he said, "Stand up." She did. "Look at me." She did that, too. Her mother stood at the washboard, back turned.

"Maria, do you think the prairie is safe for little girls?" he asked.

Maria thought very carefully about her answer. There were any number of dangers to watch out for. Rattlesnakes, if one was fool enough not to stay away from them. Prairie dogs with their holes, waiting to turn an ankle. Wolves. Bad weather. And maybe even Pawnees, if any bands of them should come by. There was even a danger, she had to admit, of actually getting lost.

In her heart, the prairie felt safe. But was it?

At last she answered, "Yes, Papa. If one is mindful."

Bram read her face, then drained the last of his tea. "Ja, Schatzie. This is all we need to know. That you will be mindful. Today, you were not. You disappoint us. Tomorrow, you will be." The way he said it, she knew it was not a prediction but a command.

Maria climbed into bed. Sleep was a long time coming. Her bottom hurt, her stomach ached, and she was truly sorry for making her parents worry. But as she lay in the low bed next to Klarina, she had a wicked thought. She knew it was wicked, but she thought it anyway. *It was worth it.*

The view from high up on Pebblehoof's back, the feel of his strong bones and powerful muscles underneath her—even with all the trouble she was in, it had been worth it.

CHAPTER 7

FOR A TIME, Maria's parents kept her close to home. After fetching her basket the next morning and bringing it home full of sagewort, she was strictly forbidden from straying beyond the homestead's marker posts. Laisa and Bram assigned her extra chores for the next two weeks, making sure to pick chores she could do nearby.

Bram rode to Columbus one day, to bring back wheat and corn for planting as soon as the weather was warm enough. He returned with the seeds, but over supper that evening, he said, "I am still worried over this railroad business."

"I am sure it is nothing," Laisa said. "Gott will watch over us."

"Well, I pray you are right. They are laying out a bridge for the trains now. But at LeClerc's, Mr. Train was complaining. This Seymour fellow, the one who came here, has moved the bridge to a new place. Now some of Mr. Train's parcels are not worth so much money."

"Och, that Mr. Train. What is it to him? He has more than any man needs already."

"Ja, but this new bridge, it is farther down on the Loup River."

"So?" asked Laisa, voicing the very question Maria was wondering. "Columbus is miles from here. What difference can it make?"

"Maybe none," Bram said, "but if Seymour does want to run the rails close by our river, it would make sense he also will move his bridge."

When supper was over, Maria cleared the table and set to washing the dishes. Another extra chore.

Laisa sat with Klarina and the barrel of willow switches—which Maria had been ordered to refill that morning—to give her younger daughter another lesson in basket weaving. If the girls learned to make good baskets, Laisa had said, they might trade them at LeClerc's dry goods store in Columbus and the girls could keep part of the money.

Maria scrubbed the tin plates. She wished she could be working on baskets instead. She stared out through the cabin's one small glass window. She could see nothing of the night outside through the reflection of the indoors in the dark glass, but she looked anyway. Pebblehoof was out there.

Somewhere out in the night, in the wide point of land between the Platte and Loup rivers, he was out there. She longed to find him and ride once more.

As soon as I can, she promised. *Just you keep your herd nearby.*

The two weeks passed slowly. When they were over, not a single weed remained in the garden. The woodpile was stacked straight and neat. The bedding was washed—not just aired, but washed and dried on an unexpectedly sunny day—and the homestead was in as fine a shape as Maria could remember.

On the last day of Maria's punishment, after the breakfast dishes were cleaned, the cow was milked, and Maria had set a loaf of bread to rise, her mother called her over.

Laisa handed Maria a brown earthenware jar, its lid sealed tight with wax. It was the last of the jars of blackberry preserves she had helped her mother put up the previous fall. "You did not thank Mr. Harper for fetching you home. Have a little something for dinner before you go, and be back by suppertime."

Suppertime! Maria smiled. Could it be? The whole afternoon, hers to do with as she pleased, without any chores. "Really, Mama?"

Laisa gave her a quick hug. "Ja, Schatzie. Go on, now."

Maria didn't need to be asked twice. She wolfed down a wedge of dry cornbread left over from the previous night's supper, took a long drink of water, and ran the whole way to Mr. Harper's.

She found him in his stable, currycombing Bessie's colt.

"Why, Maria Browning! What brings you here? Least you came in the day, this time." He let out a deep laugh.

"I came to thank you, Mr. Harper, for bringing me home before. My mother says to give you this." She held out the jar. "It's blackberry preserves."

"Well now. I declare, I'll be pleased as punch to fetch you home any time, little miss, if this is the thanks for it." He held the jar out at arm's length in front of him, looking at it. "You thank your mother for me, will you?"

Maria nodded. She half hoped he would invite her inside to have some, perhaps on a slice of bread. But he did not, and anyway she had other plans for the day. "Thank you again. I'd best be getting on."

"Yes'm. Make hay while the sun shines."

She turned to go, and was at the stable door when his voice stopped her.

"Maria?"

"Yes, sir?"

"P'haps I should have said something the other evening, but I noticed you already smelled of horse sweat when you came up. I took it for your farm horse, but now I'm not so sure." He gave her a long, appraising look.

When she did not answer, he said, "Horses are powerful creatures. Dangerous, especially if they ain't been broke. You make sure to mind yourself around horses."

Maria stammered. "I will, Mr. Harper. I will."

She ran into the prairie, pondering Mr. Harper's words. Did he somehow know what she had been up to? Did he think Pebblehoof would hurt her?

And would he? Maria wondered. She didn't think so. He seemed so gentle and kind. And after all, she had taken the pebble out of his hoof.

She tracked a wide arc across the prairie, up to the higher land where she could see better, but back in the general direction of the homestead just the same. She kept a careful eye on the sun.

Miles later, it was time to return. She was thirsty and tired. The hem of her dress was thick with briars, but she had not found the herd.

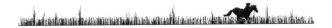

Maria settled into a routine. She found that if she was quick about her daily chores, her mother would often let her run free in the afternoons. Some days she would find the herd, other days not. Mostly not, at first, but then more often as she became accustomed to the herd's movements.

Pebblehoof always let her ride. As far as Maria could tell, he seemed to enjoy her company as much as she enjoyed his. *He must,* she reckoned. *I couldn't make him carry me if he didn't want to.*

The first few times, she only sat and let Pebblehoof wander where he would. But the more she rode, the more she found herself reading Pebblehoof's motions. She could tell, by a twitch of his ears or a ripple in his shoulder, that he was about to stop or start, turn, walk, or trot. And after that, she found she could nudge him just a little bit, to go where she wanted him to.

She knew it probably wasn't anything like what Mr. Harper said about properly breaking a horse, but it didn't seem to matter. Pebblehoof was hers, at least for as long as he cared to be. As long as the two of them understood one another, that was what mattered.

They began to ride farther, separating from the herd, and faster too. One day, she thought, *I wonder if we can ride as far as Columbus.* She wasn't exactly sure of the direction, but knew if she rode north to the Loup River—which she hadn't seen since her family had crossed it on their journey out—she could follow it downstream to find the town.

She set out, urging Pebblehoof into a gentle trot. He seemed to enjoy the excuse to run. Maria found the wind in her face, blowing her brown hair back behind her, exhilarating. She rode, marking her direction by the sun at her back, until they found the Loup River.

She looked downstream, but could not see Columbus. It might be around the next bend, or it might be miles away. She turned to face the sun, checking the time.

It was later than she thought.

"Oh, goodness!" she said, "Pebblehoof, we have to get back." She let Pebblehoof drink, and slaked her own thirst in the cool river water before mounting and urging him into the fastest run she dared.

It was a giddy, heady feeling, speeding along over the land. *Like flying.* She rode him south until they found the wagon trail, then followed it on.

The sun sunk lower. She leaned forward, almost onto Pebblehoof's strong neck, until he was galloping full out. "Good boy," she said. "You'll get me home in time, won't you?"

Minutes passed, and the racing wind drew tears to Maria's eyes. A dark line, shadowed in the afternoon light, appeared across the trail up ahead. Maria blinked her tears away and squinted to make out what it might be. Then she knew.

A stream. One she and her family had camped at, the last night on the trail before Papa picked out their quarter-section. One she and Pebblehoof had crossed earlier that afternoon.

Only then they had forded it at a walk, not a full gallop, and Maria didn't know what Pebblehoof would do.

No sooner had she wrapped her mind around the situation than they were upon it. They raced forward, coming up impossibly fast. She read a slight dip in Pebblehoof's withers and knew what he would do. *He's going to jump it!*

Maria heard a slight gap in the rhythm of Pebblehoof's gallop. Then his massive body thrust upward and they were in the air.

Maria felt herself float up off Pebblehoof's back, tilting in the air, and for the first time wished she had a saddle to hang on to. Her arms and legs flailed, her skirts catching the wind.

The stream was only two or three yards wide, and Pebblehoof cleared it easily. His hooves touched ground an instant before she crashed down onto his rump.

Her balance was lost. She flopped backwards as the bulk of him continued on and felt herself roll off his haunches. She was airborne again with nothing under her but the hard earth.

She turned full over in the air, slamming into the ground on her stomach, driving all the air from her lungs.

Maria lay there, dazed, fighting to bring breath back into her body. Her chest felt closed, her throat locked against the air. She writhed and twisted, pushing herself up onto her knees, facing the stream. Spots floated in her vision, and she heard the sound of hoofbeats.

He left me, she thought. The heartbreak of that idea broke her lungs free in a great sobbing gasp. She coughed and panted, wiping her eyes and spitting dirt out of her mouth.

Her breath wheezed loud in her throat, and blood rushed in her ears, so when the spots cleared from her eyes she was surprised to see her own shadow engulfed in a much larger one.

She turned to look at him. "You came back for me."

Pebblehoof lowered his head to nuzzle her. Maria petted his soft velvet nose, and when she was able, stood on shaking legs.

She brushed herself off. Nothing seemed broken. "I'd best get moving," she told him. He stood by her side, in the same posture he always used when he was ready for her to climb on his back.

She petted his flank and said, "Thank you, but I think I ought to walk. It's not too far, now."

She walked, and Pebblehoof walked with her in companionable silence. She turned to him and said, "I can't talk to you like my friends back home, but I reckon you're pretty good company just the same."

At last, she saw the homestead in the distance. She knew she must go on alone. "All right, boy. You go on back to your family, and I'll go to mine." Pebblehoof just stood by her.

"Go on, now. My parents can't know about you," she said. But he only looked at her. At last, she led him around the other way and slapped him on the flank. "Go on! I'll see you next time. Now go!"

Pebblehoof snorted and took a few steps away.

"That's right. Goodbye, now."

Before Pebblehoof could change his mind, she turned and ran the rest of the way home.

CHAPTER 8

THE NEXT DAY, Maria's ribs were sore from her fall. After chores, Bram saddled up Poppy for a trip to Columbus. "I will ask to see the railroad plans," he told Laisa. "I want this business settled before planting time."

Maria knew that planting would come soon, and the hard work of plowing before that. Likely she would be put to work, and for a time might lose her afternoons out with Pebblehoof. She sped through her morning chores, all the more eager to escape into the wilds.

But when she came in from milking, lugging a heavy pail of warm milk in each hand, she found Laisa inside trying to coax Klarina to drink down a mug of coneflower root tea.

Maria set down the pails. "Is she sick, Mama?"

Laisa frowned, "Ja, but she would feel better if she would drink this. Come, Klarina. Be a good girl."

Klarina fussed and squirmed, but Laisa held her tight until she had drunk the entire mug. Laisa put the girl to bed, and told her to stay there. "You rest, Kleine Maus. Maria will take care of you."

Before she could stop herself, Maria blurted out, "But Mama—"

Laisa held up a hand. "I must tend the garden and wash your papa's overalls while he is gone. You do Klarina's chores today, and tend to her."

Maria's shoulders sagged. "Yes, Mama." A whole afternoon, lost. Laisa stepped out. Klarina lay in the bed. Her rag doll was in her hands, but she was not playing with it. The doll lay as still as she did.

Maria held her hand near the cook stove, and felt that it was cool. She pulled over the ash bucket and carefully scooped the greyish white ashes from the stove. The ash bucket was nearly full.

She swept the floor. She fetched Klarina a cup of water when Klarina cried for one, and did other small jobs around the house until she couldn't think of a single thing more that needed doing.

Laisa was still hard at work in the garden. Klarina had fallen asleep, so Maria sat carefully at the foot of the bed. Lacking anything else to do, she began to weave another basket. It was easier, now that she had some practice, even though her work wasn't yet as good as her mother's.

She stopped often to gaze out the soddie's small window. It was a lovely day outside. *Perfect for a ride,* she thought. The weather was warming up, but wasn't so warm as to make her sweaty with the exertion of riding. One switch after another, the basket grew slowly in her hands.

Laisa came in for a quick dinner. She checked on Klarina, holding the backs of her fingers to the little girl's forehead, and took a moment to give Maria some help with a tricky part on the basket. Then she was out again to begin the washing.

It seemed to Maria that the day passed as slowly as any day ever had. It seemed unfair, as days up on Pebblehoof's back seemed to vanish in a moment. The only brief reprieve she had out of doors was when her mother called her outside to help hang up the washing.

Bram returned late in the afternoon, bearing a pair of rabbits he had managed to shoot on the way home.

Laisa quickly skinned them with her big kitchen knife, laying the pelts aside to clean later. "These will make nice winter boots for the girls," she said. She handed Maria a knife and the smaller of the two rabbits, and said, "Help me cut these for stew."

Maria worked by her mother's side, cutting meat away from the bones and putting it into the black iron kettle. Bram sat down with a heavy sigh, and leaned down low to stretch his back.

"Tea?" Laisa asked.

"Ja. Riding is hard for my back. Perhaps I should have walked, but I did not want to stay away the night."

Laisa handed the remains of her rabbit to Maria and set about brewing some willow bark tea. Maria was sorry her father's back hurt so much. Hers never did when she rode Pebblehoof, but it was different for her father. Something about having spent so many long hours in Chicago, stooping over something in the print shop called a Heidelberg.

When the tea was ready, Laisa asked, "How was it in Columbus?"

Bram took a long swallow. How he could stand the bitter taste without grimacing, Maria did not know.

"Och. What a waste. I should better have stayed here. Mr. Seymour was not at the railroad office. Only some rude young fellow who refused to let me see any maps or plans. I found Mr. Seymour at the new depot, but he would not talk to me. He only told me to leave, and told me a wise man would not stand in the way of progress."

"I am not sure I like the sound of that," Laisa said.

"Nein. Und the trip was hard for poor Poppy too. She is not used to such distances anymore. She should rest one day before we plow."

The stew was on to cook. Bram finished his tea and sat upright. "Ah! But the day was not all wasted." He reached into the satchel he had carried with him, and pulled out a book. "My orchardist book arrived."

"Gut," Laisa said. "When you have finished it, the girls can use it to practice their reading also."

When the food was ready, Klarina roused herself enough to have some supper with the family. The stew was rich with meat and a few wild carrots swimming in thick brown gravy.

After supper, Klarina slept. Laisa gave Maria a reading lesson, but not from Papa's new book. Laisa helped Maria read chapters from the family's Bible while Papa sat with his sore back to the warmth of the cook stove, learning how to plant and tend an orchard.

The Bible was one Bram and Laisa had brought from Germany. Maria found the German printing difficult to read, and the German language even more difficult to puzzle through.

They were reading the Book of Matthew. Had it said anything about horses, Maria might have done better. But as it did not, progress was slow.

"Mama, what's German for horse?"

"Pferd," she answered. "Why?"

"It ought to say 'Blessed are the horses,' that's all."

Laisa chuckled. "Don't be silly. It's the Bible, Schatzie."

Bram spoke up. "No, she is right. It should bless the horses. We would be lost out here without them."

CHAPTER 9

K LARINA WAS MUCH improved the next morning, but even so, Laisa kept Maria in to watch her. Papa spent the day measuring out the acres they would plow and plant, and the next day it was time for plowing.

Bram pulled Maria away from her normal chores as soon as breakfast was finished. He led her out to what he called the field, although as far as Maria could see it was the same as any other stretch of unbroken prairie.

"See here, Schatzie," he began. "Here is one corner." He pointed out a stick he had stuck upright in the ground. He led her, one by one, to the other three corners. The area inside the four stick markers was large, much larger than Laisa's garden, but didn't reach anywhere near to the corners of the family's homestead, as Maria had thought it would.

"We're not plowing all our land?" Maria asked.

Bram laughed. "Nein. Twenty acres only." He motioned to the set of markers nearest them. "Here, we will make four acres. I have paced it off. Two acres for corn, two for wheat. This will be for us, und for the animals. It is more than we need, but best to be safe for the winter, ja?"

Maria well remembered how small their meals had been, in the weeks before spring came, as Laisa rationed their supplies.

Bram went on. "The rest, also corn und wheat, to sell in Columbus. Maybe one crop will fail, and the other will succeed. I do not know. We plant two, and one should work. If both do well, we will have good fodder for Poppy. Reine will give more milk for us, too, und perhaps even we will get a pig to fatten up for hams. But we will plow these four for our family first."

They walked to the stable to fetch Poppy. Maria fed Reine some handfuls of hay while Bram fitted the harness on Poppy. The cow munched happily while Maria waited. "Mama will come milk you today, girl," Maria said. "I have to help in the field."

At last, Poppy was ready and Bram hitched her to the plow. Maria led Poppy out to the field while Bram managed the plow, keeping its curved steel blade up out of the dirt.

Poppy did not want to go. "Come on, Poppy," Maria said, tugging on Poppy's lead rope. We have to plow today."

And I want to be done with it quickly, she thought. All around her, the prairie beckoned with its wide open spaces, and the joy of riding Pebblehoof. Even if she had fallen off of him last time. *I just won't let him jump again.*

At last, they reached the field. Bram lined everything up and gave his final instructions. "Lead her straight to the next marker, then we will turn around."

Maria nodded. The lead rope hung slack between her and Poppy's bridle. At last, Papa barked out a sharp "Gee up!" and Poppy began to pull.

Maria walked ahead, holding the lead rope just tight enough

to take up the slack. Bram let the blade of the plow drop into the thick prairie sod.

Poppy whinnied at the sudden pull against her harness, and slowed down.

"Keep her going," Bram shouted. "Don't let her stop!"

Maria pulled a bit harder, watching her father wrestle the plow's two wide-set handles. He fought it as the plow bucked and jerked through the soil.

Poppy kept up for a few moments, then took a faltering step and stopped. They had barely gone ten feet.

Papa said a word in German that Maria didn't recognize. He stomped up to her.

"She just stopped, Papa," Maria said. "I was pulling just like you said."

Bram checked over Poppy's bridle and harness again, making sure all was as it should be. "Well," Bram said. "First time for all three of us."

He resumed his place at the plow, and at his command, they tried again. Poppy stopped after only five feet, holding one of her hind legs just off the ground.

"Papa, I think she's hurt!" Maria called out. She stroked Poppy's cheek while Bram came to look.

Bram pulled the hat from his head and threw it on the ground. He kicked the hat, and let out a stream of German too fast for Maria to follow.

"What's wrong, Papa?" she asked, when Bram had collected himself.

"It must have been the trip to Columbus. Too far for her in one day, und now she has come up lame. Und just at planting time!"

Poppy's foot hovered, just like Pebblehoof's had, that first day.

"I wonder if it's her foot."

Maria knelt down to look, but when she touched Poppy's leg, the horse kicked out backwards and sidestepped away. Maria scrambled back, startled.

"Get back, Maria," Bram scolded. "I'll not have you hurt, too."

"But we have to look. What if it's just a stone, stuck in her hoof?"

Bram considered. "Ja, could be. But I will look. You get back."

I've seen this before, she wanted to say. *I can fix it*, but she dared not say it.

Maria stood up and Bram took her place. Maria stepped to Poppy's head, stroking and soothing while Bram carefully inspected the hoof.

At last, he stood up. "No stone."

"There isn't?" Maria was surprised. She had been so sure. "What is it, then?"

"Ach. I have no idea. I know printing, not horses."

Bram collected his hat and sat down in the grass a little ways away. Maria sat with him.

"Didn't you do any farming back in Germany?"

"Nein. We lived in the city, there. Mainz. I learned printing in your Opa's shop. I never took a single shovel of soil in my life until we came here." He patted the earth between them with one hand.

"Well, why start a farm, then? Why didn't you just start a print shop in Columbus, or in that big city we passed through?"

"Omaha? Oh, Schatzie. I would very much have liked to do that. But we did not have enough money. Your mother and I, we saved as much as we could in Chicago. Every penny. When we had enough, we were going to do just as you said. But, Gott gave us Klarina, and for a while your mother could not work, and the money was spent on food and clothes and coal for the winter."

"Oh."

"After a time, I thought we might never leave Chicago. But then Mr. Lincoln made the Homestead Act, and so we came because the land is free. All we have to do is live on it and work on it. We had enough for that—well, perhaps not enough, but almost—so we came."

"But you still want to be a printer."

"Oh, ja. As soon as I can."

Maria thought it over. "So now we need to farm for food, and to make money so you can start your shop."

"Ja. You are a smart girl."

"But what's wrong with just having a farm?" Maria asked.

"A farm is a fine thing. But printing is..." He paused and pursed his lips in thought. "It is Kultur zu erschaffen."

Maria wasn't quite sure what he meant, but it sounded important the way he said it.

He smiled at her, and tousled her hair. "But first, we must do something about Poppy." Bram hopped up and unhitched Poppy from the plow. "Lead her back to the stables. I will go ask Mr. Harper what to do."

CHAPTER 10

BRAM FOLLOWED THE wagon trail towards Mr. Harper's place. Step by hobbling step, Maria led Poppy back to the stable. Though her father had not asked her to, she took off Poppy's harness and bridle and even managed to wrestle the heavy plow back to the stable too.

She gave Poppy oats and water, and curried her coat as best she could. Poppy wouldn't let Maria anywhere near her tender leg.

Maria combed the mare's short hair, thinking about what her father had said as they sat in the grass. She thought about how far he and her mother had come, all the way from Germany.

She didn't know what the inside of a print shop was like, but she knew not everybody could do what her father could. She was proud that he had a trade, and it made her sad that he couldn't afford to start a new shop in Columbus. *I'm going to help him,* she decided. She didn't know how, but she was determined to find a way.

At last, Poppy's coat was as clean and smooth as she could make it. When she hung up the currycomb, it was too late in the day to go out looking for Pebblehoof.

Inside, Laisa asked, "How is Poppy? Your father says she is hurt."

"It's her leg, Mama." Maria explained what had happened in the field.

Laisa shook her head. "Terrible. I do not know what we will do but say a prayer und trust Gott to provide."

Maria wished her father had asked her to come along to Mr. Harper's place. She longed to know what their neighbor would have to say.

She asked Laisa if she might run out to meet Bram on the trail, but her mother said no. "Practice your reading, Schatzie. Help Klarina with her letters, then strip some willow." She pointed to a bundle of fresh-cut switches, tied with twine next to the barrel.

All Maria could do was wait. She sat with Klarina where a square of light came in through the cabin's window, reading and drilling Klarina on what sounds the different letters make. When Klarina tired of the exercise, Maria set the book aside and began peeling long strips of willow bark from the switches.

It seemed he would never come but at last Bram returned, just before suppertime. Everyone turned to him as he came through the door.

"Well, Papa? What did Mr. Harper say?" Maria couldn't wait any longer.

Bram hung up his hat on its peg in the wall, and drank two full dippers of water from the water bucket before he answered.

"He says it could be many things. Perhaps a pulled muscle. Perhaps an abscess in her hoof. Perhaps a break in her bones."

"How do we tell which?"

Bram shrugged. "If I knew horses, I could tell. But we will

have to wait. Mr. Harper will come look at her, he says, when he can. He worries we may have to put her down."

Maria's jaw dropped. "No, Papa! You can't kill her. She'll get better."

Bram held up a hand for silence. "I will wait to hear what Mr. Harper says."

"Oh, you can't, Papa. You simply can't. She's such a sweet horse."

"Nein! I said I will wait. But if it must be done then it must be done. I will not have a lame horse eating up hay and oats, doing no work."

Laisa said, "Perhaps we can borrow a horse."

"Ach. I asked. I hate to ask for such things, but I asked. Mr. Harper has his own plowing to attend to. He cannot spare a horse. If only we…"

He didn't finish, but Maria knew what he was thinking. *If only we hadn't sold Jess.* They had come to the prairie with two horses. But when fall came, they hadn't put away enough stores for the winter. Bram had sold Jess to a man in Columbus to buy the provisions they had survived on until spring. There hadn't been any other choice. They'd had to.

"What are we going to do, Bram?" Laisa asked.

Bram pounded his fist against the wall. "I don't know! The Devil take that Mr. Seymour und his railroad!"

Laisa gasped and covered Klarina's ears. "Bram!"

Bram's face was tight. "Ja, ja. I know. It is my fault too. I should have plowed, instead of wasting a day going to Columbus."

"Can we buy another?"

"Another horse? So expensive. An old nag, perhaps, if we had one hundred dollars. Waste of money. A good horse is perhaps one hundred und fifty dollars. We do not have it."

"The girls and I can weave baskets. We can make some money that way."

Maria's heart rose. *Yes.* She would weave a dozen baskets, even a hundred, if it meant keeping Poppy.

"Ja, but not in time to plant. That will be too late. The rains will come soon. Seeds must be in the ground. If we miss the rain, we will have no crop. The ground must be turned, or the grass will choke everything."

And just as quickly, Maria's hopes slipped away. Papa was right. Her basketry was improving, but was not near so fine as her mother's. By the time she was that good, it would be much too late for planting.

If only they hadn't sold Jess. If only there was another horse. *I know another horse,* Maria thought. But no. She couldn't tell her parents about Pebblehoof. She couldn't even be sure of finding him on any given day, much less that he would plow for her.

She said a prayer for Poppy's quick recovery and finished stripping the willow.

MORNING CAME, AND Bram went out to check on Poppy. It seemed forever until he returned. When he stepped back inside the soddie, his face was grim. He reached for his rifle.

Maria screamed. "No, Papa! You can't!" She flew from her seat at the table, clinging to his arm.

"Do you think I want to?" Bram roared. He shook his arm, breaking Maria's hold, and she stumbled to the floor. "She is not better, she is worse! She will not move even one step."

"But you promised, Papa. You promised you'd wait for Mr. Harper. He'll come, I know he will. You'll see."

Bram began loading the rifle. "Und how long am I to wait?

Maybe he will come this morning. Maybe not until next week. How long do I feed a lame horse? Already I do not know where we will find the money to buy a new horse. I should make it worse feeding a lame one?"

Tears streamed down Maria's face. Klarina clung to Laisa's skirts, hiding her face away from her father. Bram took the cap off his powder horn and filled the rifle's flash pan. He fitted a small square of cloth around a round bullet, tucked them into the end of the barrel, and rammed it all the way down with a metal rod.

He marched outside, slamming the cabin door. No one spoke a word. Maria's heart raced. Papa would be at the stable in moments. Maria knew she had to act.

She threw herself out the door, into the bright morning light. Bram was just at the stable door. Maria ran as fast as her legs could move her. "Papa, no!" she yelled.

Bram neither turned at the sound of her voice nor stopped. He pulled back the hammer on the rifle and stepped into the stable. Maria ran on without thinking. She flew through the stable door and jumped between her father and Poppy, as Bram was raising the gun.

"Maria! Get out."

The words rushed out of her. "I'll get you a horse, Papa. I can do it. A good horse. A strong horse. Just don't shoot Poppy, please don't shoot Poppy."

"Do not be foolish, girl. Where will you get a horse? Now move. Poppy is suffering. It is a mercy."

Maria held her ground. She looked her father straight in the eyes. "I can so get a horse. You promised you won't shoot Poppy, at least not until Mr. Harper can have a look at her. Just keep your promise, please, and I'll get you a horse."

Bram lowered the gun and pulled at his beard. "Heavens,

Maria. I think you are serious."

Maria only stood guard in front of Poppy, her arms spread out as if to hide the mare behind her.

"Come inside," Bram said. "You will explain, and we will see what your mother has to say."

Maria did not move until her father carefully lowered the hammer on the rifle. He stepped outside, and she followed.

She swallowed hard. Her secret would be gone, and she did not know what would come of it. She only prayed they would agree.

CHAPTER 11

WHEN THEY ENTERED the cabin, Laisa said, "What is it? I did not hear a shot."

"I did not shoot," Bram explained. "Your daughter says she can get me a horse."

Laisa looked at Maria with wide eyes. "What is this?"

Maria took a deep breath. "There is a prairie horse," she began. "I call him Pebblehoof."

She told them the whole story, starting with how the herd had stampeded past her that first day, destroying that basket but leaving her untouched.

"So that is what happened to the basket," Laisa said.

She told them about Pebblehoof limping up to her, and how she had removed the stone from his hoof.

"So that is why you wanted to check Poppy's hoof," Bram said.

She told them about riding Pebblehoof for the first time, and how the herd had led her far out past Mr. Harper's place.

"So that is why you were so late. Maria, what were you thinking?" Laisa asked. "Wild horses? This is dangerous. It is a miracle you have not been hurt."

"Well, I haven't been. I can ride him just fine." She decided not to tell them about the time Pebblehoof jumped over the stream.

Bram's arms were folded, and she could see the muscles flexing in his jaw even under his beard. "Is that all?"

"Yes, Papa."

Bram turned to Laisa, who only shook her head and threw up her hands.

"I do not like you doing this," Bram said. "Your mother is right. It is dangerous. You could fall. Get hurt somewhere out there," he waved his hand in a broad sweep, "und we would never find you. I will decide your punishment later. Why did you not tell us this, that day you were late? You must never lie to us, Maria."

Maria's face flashed hot. "I didn't lie! I—" Bram stopped her with a look. She knew she hadn't lied, exactly. *I just didn't tell the whole truth.* "Yes, Papa. But can I go find Pebblehoof, please?"

Bram stroked his beard again. "I do not like it. A wild horse? Will he even take the plow?"

"I know he will, Papa. He'll take the plow if I'm with him, I just know it."

He grunted. "If there were any other choice…"

She knew he was almost convinced, but not quite. If only he saw Pebblehoof, just one time, Bram would know how strong he was. But if Maria couldn't convince him to let her go, he'd never see. Maria knew what she had to do. *Say it in German.*

"Pebblehoof ist…" She thought hard, trying to remember a word she had heard her father say once. "Er ist baumstark."

Bram and Laisa burst out laughing.

Maria's face fell. "What? He is! Just wait, you'll see."

Bram managed to say, "Ja, what else would he be?" before

doubling over, coughing with the laughter. Maria's face burned with embarrassment.

Laisa was the first to recover. "Maria, baumstark means strong as a horse. You have said your horse is as strong as a horse."

Maria's blush only deepened. "Oh."

When Bram could breathe again, Maria asked, "Well, Papa? Can I go?"

Bram gave her a smile. "Sehr wohl, Maria. You must still have a punishment, but ja, we will try your baumstarkes Pferd."

"And you won't shoot Poppy?"

"Perhaps. If you can find this Pebblehoof of yours, und if he will plow like you say, then I will wait for Mr. Harper to tell us if anything can be done."

Maria didn't hesitate. Before her parents could change their minds, and although she hadn't even started her morning chores, she raced outside to find Pebblehoof.

MARIA RAN, PRAYING she could find Pebblehoof—and quickly— now that she actually needed him. But it had been three days since her last ride. Her ribs still twinged from when she had fallen, and knifed at her as she ran.

Three whole days. *They could be anywhere*, Maria realized. In three days, the herd could easily wander miles and miles away. She made for the high part of the prairie between the Platte and Loup rivers.

She was panting and sorely out of breath, when she reached the high grass. She turned slowly, looking carefully, both nearby and as far away as she could see. She turned the full circle, but did not spot them. *I can't give up*, she told herself. As long as she was still looking, Poppy would be spared.

She had come a long ways from the homestead. It would be midday well before she returned. Klarina would be sitting down to eat a little something. Laisa would be deciding whether to set out a plate for Maria, or to wait. Maria could imagine her mother holding the plate, then putting it back, empty. Why dirty a plate when Maria wasn't there? She regretted not having thought to bring anything with her for a dinner.

She stood in the grass, wondering what to do. *Maybe if I can think like a horse.* She tried it. What would Pebblehoof do? It was morning. She assumed the herd slept at night, just like Poppy. They would wake. They would be hungry, just like she was.

Only for the herd, breakfast would be all around them. Grass as far as the eye could see.

Maria swallowed, her throat dry from running. *They'd be thirsty, too,* she realized. They would have to go down to the water in the morning. But which river? If she knew which one, she could maybe follow along it and find them.

Although she did not know the area well, she decided to try the Loup River, to the north. The Platte was bigger, but the wagon trail ran along it, and there were more houses and people. She reckoned the herd would stay mostly away from it, when they could.

Her strength recovered, Maria turned north. The land rolled in its pattern of soft waves, sloping gently down as she went. The sun passed high noon, and Maria's stomach growled. She stopped at a place where a small, fresh spring bubbled up out of the ground, and drank as much as her stomach would hold. The water eased her hunger somewhat, though she knew it wouldn't last.

She stopped now and again to listen, and called out for Pebblehoof. She wished she had taught him to come at a whistle, and decided to do so as soon as she could manage.

In the early afternoon, she stopped at a muffled sound coming from up ahead. She strained her ears, until she heard it again. *Horses!* She looked, but saw nothing. But she had heard them, she was sure of it. She ran onward, towards the sound.

The grass grew taller here, almost up to her shoulders, and so it was that she did not see the cliff until she was upon it.

One moment she was in grass, the next, space opened up before her and the land fell away from her feet. Her weight broke the soil at the cliff's edge, and she fell down, arms flailing.

She slid down the steep dirt slope, and only as her shoulders reached the break did she manage to clutch her fingers into a clump of prairie grass.

The tuft's strong roots held firm, stopping her slide.

Maria said a quick prayer, and pulled herself hand over hand back up to the top.

She had stumbled upon a gully, a sharp ravine cut into the land by the spring's snowmelt. But that was not all she saw. Below her, the gully scooped its way down to the Loup, and there she saw them.

The herd was at the water's edge, heads down to drink. They were stretched out in a line along the bank, wider than she could see through the narrow mouth of the gully.

"Pebblehoof!" she called out. But none of the horses turned to look. *I have to get down there*, she thought. *Find him.*

She looked again at the steep gully wall. It was almost a sheer drop, where she sat. But farther down, on her right, it seemed less treacherous.

She moved there, and eased her feet over the edge. She didn't fancy her chances of climbing down, but reckoned if she was careful she could slide down on her bottom.

She lowered herself down, down, her arms bearing more and more of her weight. Below, the herd paid her no mind. There was nothing for it but to let go.

Instantly, she was in motion, careening downward. Her heels kicked at the ground, her hands dug into it, trying to slow her progress.

One foot caught on a rock jutting out of the dark soil. It was only for an instant, but it was enough to upset her balance. Maria tumbled, tucking her head under an instant before her face met the dirt. She rolled like a barrel. Earth and sky flashed in her vision. She felt a pain in one hand before thumping to a stop at the bottom.

She gained her breath and checked herself over. Her dress, her hair, were covered with dirt. The heel of one hand was scraped through the skin. But nothing seemed to be broken.

She pushed herself up onto her knees, then stood to look for Pebblehoof.

From the bottom of the ravine, at the place where it opened up onto the river bank, she could see the whole herd. She walked along behind them, careful to keep some distance from their hind legs, talking softly the whole while.

At last, a head popped up, showing her the familiar white blaze.

"There you are!" She motioned to him. "Come on, boy. Oh, I'm so glad I found you."

Pebblehoof made his way out of the line, away from the water, and came over to her. She touched his withers and he lowered down so she could mount.

When he stood up again, she said "I hope you know the way out of here, because I don't think we can go back up the way I came down."

She urged Pebblehoof into a walk, then gave him his head. He led them upriver, and soon they came to a place where the gullies faded out and the rolling grass reached almost down to the water's edge.

"Good boy." They gathered speed into a trot, then a run, and were soon flying across the prairie once more. Maria felt her cheeks might break from smiling, but she did not let Pebblehoof go into a full gallop this time. She did not want to fall again.

At last, she saw the homestead come into view. She checked the sun. It was two, perhaps three o'clock. The day was mostly gone.

She slowed them down to a walk, letting Pebblehoof cool down as they approached. Laisa was in the garden, pulling weeds, and Bram was splitting wood.

"Mama, Papa, I found him!"

She rode him in at a walk, as her parents ran to meet them. Pebblehoof shied away from them, and they stopped a few feet away. She stroked his neck. "Easy, boy. They're my herd. They won't hurt you any."

Pebblehoof settled. Maria could not help but smile, looking down at her parents from her perch on Pebblehoof's broad back.

Laisa ran her eyes up and down her daughter, and said, "Maria, what happened to you? You are filthy!"

"It's nothing, Mama. I'm fine. I'll wash my dress, don't worry." She rubbed at the spot on her hand, now sticky with dirt and blood.

Bram looked Pebblehoof over for a long minute. "Ja," he admitted. "This is a fine horse."

Maria couldn't help but say, "I told you he was."

"What do you call him?" Bram asked. Maria told him, and he said, "Ja, Pebblehoof. Come then. It is late. Let us see if he will take the plow."

CHAPTER 12

MARIA'S STOMACH WAS hollow. She longed to go inside for something to eat, but she dared not leave Pebblehoof alone. She wasn't sure she should even climb down off his back, for fear he might run away. *He might, anyway,* she thought, but she stayed mounted up and walked Pebblehoof over to the stable.

Bram came out with the harness and bridle. "Come down, Schatzie, while I put this on him."

Pebblehoof knelt at her signal, and Maria slipped off his back. She stood on the other side from Bram, but kept a firm hold on Pebblehoof's mane with one hand.

Bram stepped up. Maria stroked his neck, and kept up a stream of soothing words. But when Bram laid the collar around Pebblehoof's neck and shoulders, the horse jerked. He whinnied, and shook his neck so hard Maria lost her grip and Bram had to grab for the collar.

Maria latched onto his mane again, as fast as she could. "Come on, Pebblehoof. We need to do this. Oh, I know you don't understand. But it's important."

Pebblehoof gave her a look she was certain meant he was mad at her.

"Please, boy. It's just for a little while. Won't you do it for me? This little collar won't hurt you."

Bram tried again, slower this time. It took three tries, by which time Maria was almost in tears. But at last Bram fitted the collar around Pebblehoof's neck and cinched up the strap to make it snug.

Maria looked at the remaining pile of tackle; straps and buckles, pads and chains, bit and bridle. Her heart sank. *He won't take it all.*

"Papa," she asked, "Do we really need all that?"

Bram took off his hat and fanned himself, then set the hat back on his head. "No. It would be better, but we can leave some off. Let us put on the bridle, so you can lead him, and that will be enough."

"Alright."

But Pebblehoof would not take the bridle. The first time, Pebblehoof knocked it out of Bram's hands with a flick of his head. The second time, he stamped and shook and nipped at Bram's hand. The third time, Pebblehoof whinnied and reared up. Maria clung on with both arms around his neck, her eyes squeezed tightly shut.

It took a long time to calm Pebblehoof down. Bram's face was a stony mask. "He will not do it. This is a demon horse, Maria. Get the collar off and send him away."

"No!" Maria cried. "He will, Papa. He just doesn't understand, that's all. Let me—" She thought hard. There had to be something. Some way to make this work. Some way to give Poppy a chance. "What if we tie a lead rope to the bottom of the collar? Lead him that way?"

Bram sighed. "Ja. Very well. I do not like it, but we must plow somehow."

Bram fetched a length of rope from the stable, but he let Maria tie it on. This, Pebblehoof did not seem to mind. All that was left was to attach the plow. Maria stood by Pebblehoof's head, keeping eye contact with him and talking to him, while Bram fixed the long traces from the collar to the plow.

At last, they were ready.

Maria stood in front of Pebblehoof, the lead rope coiled in her hand. Bram stood behind the plow, gripping its handles. Maria made the soft clicking sound, gave a gentle pull on the rope, and Pebblehoof started walking.

"Good boy!" She wished she had a carrot or an apple to give him, but the carrots weren't big enough to pick and she hadn't seen an apple in months. Praise would have to be enough.

They walked slowly out to the pasture, giving Pebblehoof time to accustom himself to the feel of the plow behind him. They lined up at the near corner of the field.

"What now?" Maria asked.

Bram said, "I put the plow down, und you walk him straight down the line. You see the other marker, ja?"

Maria nodded.

"Gut. Walk him straight past it. I will lift up the plow at the end of the row. We will turn around, und come back down the next. Make the rows about so far apart." He held his hands out for her to see.

"All right." Maria took a deep breath. "You hear that, Pebblehoof? You be good for me now. It's just walking."

They started again. Bram lowered the plow down to the earth. The blade bit into the prairie sod, and the traces jerked taut. Pebblehoof nickered and took a small step backward. The lead rope yanked too, pulling out of Maria's hand with a rasp across the spot she had skinned earlier.

Maria cried out and held her hand. Pebblehoof, thankfully, stood where he was.

Maria held her injured hand with the other, but forced calm into her voice. "It's all fine, Pebblehoof. You have to pull. That's the job. But it's just walking."

They started again. Maria moved to the other side of him, though, so as to hold the lead rope with her other hand.

It took two more false starts before Pebblehoof had the feel of it, and then they were plowing. Maria walked ahead, slow and steady. Row by row, they made their way across the field.

Maria stole a glance backward, now and again, to see the soil turn over. It was mesmerizing to watch the green of the grass curve up over the metal blade, tipping into a spill of black topsoil.

Back and forth they went. For a while, Klarina came out to watch. She wanted to follow along with Maria, but Bram wouldn't allow it and made her stay behind the plow.

They worked until the sun went down. Laisa called them in to supper. Bram sent Klarina in, but refused to stop. Maria's stomach growled fiercely, but she did not complain. They kept on until the light was too dim to work.

Maria had long since lost count of the rows, when Bram called, "Lead us back now. Is enough for today." She turned them towards the stable, and felt the change in Pebblehoof's gait when Bram lifted the plow blade back out of the soil.

They had made good progress, but had finished perhaps only one of the four acres Bram had marked out. There was a lot of field left to plow.

When they reached the stable, Maria stepped in front of Pebblehoof. "Whoa, boy. That's good." Pebblehoof stopped.

Bram strode up to her, then leaned backwards with his hands on his hips. He let out a grunt as he stretched his back.

"Good work, Schatzie." She could see him smiling in the twilight. Behind him, the evening star shone in the blue-black sky. "Hold him here while I take off the collar, then put him in with Poppy. Don't let go. We can't have you gone half the day tomorrow to find him."

Maria handed her father the lead rope and held once more onto Pebblehoof's mane while Bram unhooked the traces and removed the collar.

"Come on, boy," she said. Pebblehoof followed her a step or two before balking at the stable door. It was dusky twilight outside, but pitch black inside, and Pebblehoof would not step inside.

"I know, boy. I wouldn't want to go into that dark stable either. But come on. Come in and meet Poppy." Maria tugged and encouraged him, but he wouldn't budge.

Maria asked, "Does he have to go in there? Can't we just put him in the paddock?"

Bram shook his head. "Nein. He will only jump out. But I have an idea." He fetched a lantern from the cabin, and hung it from a high rafter inside the stable. He gathered up a feed bag, and dropped a heaping scoop of oats into it.

Maria thought of the bridle. *He'll never wear that*, she thought, and said so.

"Nein, but you will," Bram said. He draped the bulky feed bag over Maria's shoulder so she could reach it with her free hand. "Give him some," he said.

She scooped a handful of oats from the bag and gingerly brought them up to Pebblehoof's mouth. Pebblehoof sniffed, then took a bite. His lips brushed Maria's hand. She squealed and flinched, dropping the rest of the oats.

"Try again," Bram said. "Let him smell, und lead him inside."

Maria thought it over and nodded. She held up another hand-ful, just beyond Pebblehoof's nose.

"Come inside, boy. Lots of good oats inside. I know you're hungry too."

Pebblehoof took a step forward and she let him have the oats, steeling herself not to flinch. She held up another handful, but this time walked forward with him, keeping the oats just out of reach until she had walked him all the way inside. She put him in the empty stall, where Jess had once lived.

Bram closed the stall gate behind them. Pebblehoof whinnied and stamped at the sound of the closing gate.

"It's just for tonight, boy. We'll be back outside in the morn-ing. You'll see."

"Leave it closed," Bram told her. Maria nodded. She could duck under easily enough, but Pebblehoof could not. "Give him food and water, tend to Poppy, then come in for supper. You must always tend your horses before yourself."

"Yes, Papa," she answered, as Bram stepped out of the stable.

Maria was glad to do it. Maria filled Pebblehoof's feed trough, spread fresh hay in his stall, and filled his water pail. She did the same for Poppy, who still held her back hoof up off the ground. Bram had been right. Poppy seemed worse than before.

When the work was done, Maria headed for the stable door.

Pebblehoof whinnied at her. She stepped back into his stall, stroked his mane, and said, "I need to go have my own supper, you know. I haven't eaten anything since breakfast!"

But Pebblehoof wouldn't let her leave. Every time she moved to go out of the stall, Pebblehoof objected. He became more and more agitated with every attempt. At last, Maria gave up.

"Very well, then. I suppose I'll have to stay with you tonight.

But if that's the way it's going to be, you're going to have to share your supper."

Maria was glad for the oats, although she felt hungry enough to eat hay. Even so, the oats were hard knots between her teeth, and it took ages even to get a single handful down.

After a long while, Bram returned.

"Papa, I can't leave him. He's too scared without me."

Bram nodded, and eyed the oats in her hand. "That is horse food, Maria. It is bad enough riding a wild horse. I will not have you eating like one as well. I will send your mother with a proper supper and a blanket."

"Thank you, Papa." Laisa came soon after, with a bowl of bean stew in which Maria found a bit of salt pork. It was delicious, and did much to fill the hollowness inside her.

Maria yawned. It had been a long, tiring day. She made up a thicker bed of straw in one corner of the stall, and brought the lantern down from the rafter. She lay down, pulled the blanket over herself, and blew out the light.

"Good night, Pebblehoof," she said. "Good night, Poppy."

MARIA WOKE EARLY. Pebblehoof was awake. She sat up and brushed away a few pieces of straw that clung to her cheek. Pebblehoof had turned around, and had his head out over the gate to the stall.

"I think we should stay here, boy. I'm sure Papa will come soon." With no collar and lead rope, Maria wasn't at all sure she could keep Pebblehoof from bolting, if she dared lead him outside on her own.

She enticed him back to the feed trough with more oats, wishing she had something to eat herself.

Papa came a while later. Klarina was right behind him, bearing a plate of griddle-cakes drizzled with honey.

"Eat quickly, while I put on the harness," he said. "We must begin work at once."

Maria stayed by Pebblehoof's head. She shoved griddle-cakes into her mouth with one hand and stroked Pebblehoof's nose with the other. It went better than before, with only one false start before Bram had the collar in place.

Bram fed and watered Poppy while Maria led Pebblehoof out to the field. When Bram joined them, Maria asked after Poppy.

Bram shook his head. "She is just as bad as before. Maria, I know it is hard, but we cannot keep her if she will not get well."

Maria's eyebrows pulled together. "But Mr. Harper hasn't come yet!"

"Und we cannot wait forever. When we are done with the plowing, I must—"

"No!" Maria screamed. "You can't! You said if Pebblehoof would plow, you wouldn't put her down. You said, Papa. You promised."

"Schatzie," Bram said, and his voice was much softer than she expected. "Poppy is suffering. I am no horseman, but I can see she has much pain. It will be a kindness. It is no life for her, only standing in her stall, unable even to make one step. Now take your place, and let us plow."

Maria wanted to scream, to cry, to argue with him. But a hard knot in her throat kept her from saying anything. *Perhaps he is right*, she thought, but prayed he wasn't.

Soon they were plowing once more. It was faster now. Pebblehoof knew his part, and it seemed to Maria he understood that the faster he went, the sooner it would be over.

Up and down the rows they went. Maria was glad to walk ahead, where Bram would not see her tears. She was ashamed to cry and kept her voice silent, but she could not stop her eyes from watering so.

The sun rose high, and when they had finished the second acre, Laisa came out with two buckets. One held a light dinner, the other held water for Pebblehoof.

"Half done," said Bram. "We will finish by supper." Sweat dripped down his face and off the tips of his beard. Maria was warm, but not tired. She was glad to have the easy part, just walking.

They ate quickly, then back to work. *Two more acres*, Maria thought, *and we'll be done*. Two more acres, and Bram would fetch his rifle from inside the cabin.

Maria found herself walking slower. *Poor Poppy.* But her father soon noticed, and barked at her to speed up. She did, and Pebblehoof gamely kept up the pace. She stole many glances down the wagon trail as the afternoon wore on, but Mr. Harper did not appear.

Try as she might, she could not keep her mind off of Poppy. Papa would make it quick, she knew that. But it was still sad. And what would they do with Poppy afterwards?

No sooner had she thought the question, than she knew the answer. She didn't want to know, but she did. *We'll have to butcher her and put up the meat.*

The thought of eating poor Poppy, who had come with them all the way from Chicago, turned Maria's stomach. She knew it would be a sin to waste that much meat — and foolish besides; the memory of the hungry times at the end of winter was still fresh in her mind — but just the same she couldn't bear to think of it.

They plowed on, every row bringing the moment closer. *At least it will be over.*

The third acre fell to furrows by midafternoon. Then, when

they were halfway through the fourth, with perhaps only an hour's work left to do, Maria caught sight of something on the trail. Just a glimpse, as she turned Pebblehoof around at the end of a row.

Leading Pebblehoof down the next row, she turned to see who it was and veered to the side.

"Maria! Walk straight!" Bram ordered.

She whipped her eyes forward and forced herself to be patient.

When they turned once more to face the trail, Maria took a good long look. It was a man riding a horse. He was closer now, and by the time they reached the end of the row, she could tell who it was.

"Papa, he's here," she shouted. "It's Mr. Harper."

Maria jumped and waved one arm. Mr. Harper waved back.

"Alright," said Bram. "We stop for a moment." Bram dropped the plow, wiped his forehead, and walked out to meet their neighbor. "You stay with Pebblehoof."

Mr. Harper hopped lightly down from his horse and shook Bram's hand. Maria watched as the two men walked up together.

When they reached her, Mr. Harper tipped his hat to her. "Good afternoon, Miss Browning. It is delightful to see you again."

Maria curtseyed, as best she could while holding Pebblehoof's lead rope. She caught Mr. Harper's eye, begging him with a look not to say anything about that night, and how he'd smelled horse on her. She knew her father wouldn't like to learn Mr. Harper had known about Pebblehoof before.

Mr. Harper inspected Pebblehoof up and down. "Whoo-ee," he said. "That is a fine stallion, iff'n I do say. Your father tells me you wrangled this'n off the prairie yourself. That so, Miss?"

Relief washed through her. "Yes, sir."

"Well I declare, you German girls have a trick or two tucked into your skirt pockets, ain'tcha?" He gave a sidelong look at Pebblehoof's bare hindquarters. "He's hitched up a mite unusual, though."

"I know," Bram said. "This is all the tack he would take. But it seems to be enough."

Mr. Harper tipped his head just to one side. "Wouldn't do for a wagon, but for a plow, I reckon so."

Maria could bear it no longer. "Please, Mr. Harper. You have to look at Poppy. You have to do something for her, oh please."

Mr. Harper lowered down on one knee to look her in the eye. "Now, little miss, if there's anything can be done, I'll do it. But I cain't promise you nothing. You understand?"

Maria nodded.

Bram said, "I must continue to plow. Would you oblige me to look at the horse yourself?"

Mr. Harper stood up and put the hat back on his head. "I'd be happy to. You get on with your plowing, and I'll come hollerin' iff'n I need anything."

Bram and Mr. Harper shook hands again. Maria tugged Pebblehoof's lead rope, and they plowed while Mr. Harper led Bessie on down to the stable.

Maria longed to be inside with Mr. Harper. It had been bad enough waiting so long for him to arrive. Now that he was here, she found waiting to learn the outcome even worse.

They had plowed only two rows when Mr. Harper came out of the stable. He loped over to them at a slow trot.

"Rest easy, Mr. Browning. Your mare's only got an abscess."

Maria and Bram asked at almost the same instant, "What's that?"

"It's just a sour spot, up under her hoof. It pains her something awful, but it's not anything too terrible serious. I'll drain it and she'll be fine in a few days, God willin'. I could do with another pair of strong hands for the job, though."

Maria couldn't help herself. She knew it wasn't at all proper, but she flung herself at Mr. Harper and hugged him around his barrel of a chest.

"Oh, now," Mr. Harper said. "No need for all that. It's no miracle. She probably bumped it, maybe knocked her hoof on a rock just so, and the bruise went sour. It happens, time to time. Now, let's lead this beast of yours up to the paddock so he don't make no trouble with that plow, and we'll get your mare sorted out."

"Danke, Herr Harper," Papa said. He grabbed for Mr. Harper's hand and shook it yet again.

They drove Pebblehoof and the plow over by the paddock. Maria tied the lead rope to the paddock fence. Mr. Harper sent her to fetch a tub of fresh water and Epsom salts, while he and Bram went into the stable.

Maria ran inside to fetch one of Laisa's big tin wash tubs. She brought it to the stable, and ran buckets back and forth from the well until the tub was full. On the way with the last bucket, she heard the awful, unearthly sound of Poppy screaming.

She ran into the stable, sloshing half the bucket on her skirts. Mr. Harper was scooping water with his hand, rinsing Poppy's hoof, which Bram was holding with all his might.

Maria smelled a foul odor at Poppy's stall. A knife with a wicked, curved blade lay on the ground by Mr. Harper's foot.

"Quick, girl," he said. "Empty your bucket and mix in those salts."

Maria did as she was told. Then she and Mr. Harper lugged the heavy basin under Poppy's foot.

"Set her hoof down into it, Mr. Browning."

Bram lowered Poppy's foot slowly into the water. She flinched for just a moment, but then set the foot fully down. For the first time in days, she put her foot down.

"There she goes," Mr. Harper said. His eyes beamed. "The salt will draw out the rest of the bad blood. You change that water every day for three days, then let it stay dry."

"Ja, we do that," Bram said.

"Can you sew, little miss?"

"Yes, sir," Maria said.

"Good. You get some scraps of canvas or burlap from your mother, or even leather, and you sew up a boot to cover that foot once it's dry. It'll heal, but you have to keep it clean. Let her walk in the paddock as she will, but keep that hoof clean. Just keep the boot on till she wears through it."

"Ja," Bram said again. "We do that."

"Another week, I reckon, she'll be right as rain."

"Danke, Mr. Harper. You have saved..." Bram paused. "Everything. You must stay to supper, ja?"

"Another time, Mr. Browning. I need to get back. My cows'll be waiting. How's about Sunday? I hain't had a home-cooked Sunday dinner in, land sakes, I cain't even recollect."

Bram agreed, and Mr. Harper rode on his way home. When he was off, Bram said, "Come, Schatzie. We must finish our work, too."

Maria stood at the paddock fence, untying Pebblehoof's lead rope. She was surprised at the feel of her father's hand on her shoulder, and a kiss upon her head.

"Und danke, Maria," he said. "You were right that I should wait. You are my smart girl. What would I do without you?"

Maria did not know what to say, so she only said, "Bitte sehr, Papa."

They had lost some time with Mr. Harper's visit, so the last acre wasn't plowed until after sunset. Bram unhitched the plow. Maria stood by Pebblehoof's head, waiting for her father to remove the collar. She stroked Pebblehoof's neck, wishing the garden's carrots were ready to pluck. *He deserves a treat,* she thought.

Bram stood at Pebblehoof's side. He laid one hand on Pebblehoof's flank. "Good job, Maria. You have saved everything, also, with your good horse."

As before, Maria stood with her fingers laced through Pebblehoof's mane, steadying him while Bram took off the collar.

"He is ein gutes Arbeitspferd," Bram went on. "I think we keep him, ja?"

Maria's jaw dropped. "What?"

"He is good, ah, horse for working. Ja, that is it. We will keep him."

A pit opened up in Maria's middle. *Keep him at the homestead?* She could not imagine taking him away from his herd. His family. She imagined him in Jess's old stall, all the time, and the way he would look at her whenever she came into the stable.

"Papa, no! He's a wild horse! We can't keep him." *He would hate me.* "He's free."

"He is a horse, Maria. Gott put animals on the earth to serve us. Mind me, girl, und take him into his stall now."

Maria felt her forehead wrinkling, bunching up into lines like the furrows in the fresh-plowed fields. *It wasn't God,* she thought, *it was me.* But she would never dare say such a thing out loud.

"Now, Maria." There was nothing soft in Bram's voice this time.

Maria took a deep breath. *No more rides, either.* "I'm sorry, Pebblehoof. Come on, boy."

She tugged at his mane, leading him away from the paddock fence. But when she turned him towards the stable, Pebblehoof balked. He planted his legs to the ground and stopped.

"I know you don't like it in there. I'm sorry, but you have to."

She patted the curve of his neck. "Please."

But Pebblehoof would not be moved. Bram said, "Wait. I will get the feedbag."

Maria heard him in the dark stable, scooping oats into the bag. He emerged a minute later, holding it out to Maria.

At the sight of the feed bag, Pebblehoof neighed and bucked, breaking Maria's grip on his mane.

"Grab him!" Bram shouted. The bag fell from his hand.

Bram lunged, and Maria lunged too, but Pebblehoof reared up. He towered over them, his front hooves pawing the air in front of her face.

She scrambled backwards, her foot catching on the back of her dress. She fell into a heap. Pebblehoof leapt over her, bolting away into the night.

Bram was at her side in an instant, his hand grabbing her by the arm. He hauled her up to her feet. "Ach, Maria!" Bram shouted. "Why did you let go?"

"I didn't," Maria shot back. "I was doing what you said, but he's too smart for that. Why, Papa? Why did you make me do that?" She felt the hot flush in her cheeks, and was glad for the concealing darkness. "Now he's gone and I'll probably never see him again."

"Ja, well, gut!" Bram said. He glanced in the direction Pebblehoof had gone. "It is for the best anyhow. You should not ride that Teufelspferd to begin with."

"He's not, Papa! He was my friend. Oh, I hate it here!" She swept both hands out wide from her sides, taking in the whole of the prairie. "Why did we have to come here, anyway? I don't have anybody else out here. All I had was Pebblehoof, and now — And now he hates me! We should have just stayed in Chicago."

Bram's hand flew up, his palm flat. Maria braced for the blow she knew was coming, the slap across her face she knew she deserved for talking back.

"Go ahead, then!" she shouted.

But the blow did not come. They stood like statues in the deepening twilight.

At last, Bram said, "When you may be civil, you may apologize and come in to supper." He turned on his heel and marched into the cabin.

I'd rather eat oats! Maria turned on her heel, and marched into the stable.

He yelled back at her from the doorway of the soddie, "Und you will leave that horse alone after this, do you hear?"

All the fire snuffed out of her. She wanted to run inside, to apologize at once, beg her father to take it back. Never see Pebblehoof again? *How can I bear it?* Tears stung in her eyes and her throat closed tight and hard.

She stood, frozen, at the door to the dark stable. She wanted to turn toward the house, but could not make herself do it. She felt her way through the dark stable, to Jess's stall. The blanket was still there. She curled up on her hay bed, and after a time, she calmed down.

She would eventually have to apologize to Papa. There would be no getting around that. But she knew something else, too. *Pebblehoof's my only friend.* Although her father had forbidden her, and although she always tried to be obedient and make him proud, in this one thing she knew she could not obey. *I'll find him again,* she promised herself. *I need him.*

CHAPTER 13

THE NEXT DAYS were occupied with planting. Bram had Maria out in the freshly-plowed fields, helping to sow wheat and plant hills of corn. Maria apologized to her father, and although he said nothing about it, Bram seemed to have forgiven her for Pebblehoof's escape. For her part, Maria made a point not to mention Pebblehoof at all. *Let them think I have forgotten him,* she thought.

Mr. Harper came to supper that Sunday, a fiddle-case tucked under his arm. He entertained the family with songs long into the evening. At last, as Maria stifled a yawn, he said, "I surely do regret I hain't got a proper table and chairs to sit you four alongside m'self, so's I could repay your hospitality in kind. Soon as I do, you count on coming down." Bram was happy to accept his invitation.

Bram and Maria finished planting the four acres the next day, under darkening clouds. No sooner had they come in for supper than the rain began, just as Bram said it would. Bram stood in the doorway of the soddie, staring into the warm, gray afternoon, looking out at the acres they hadn't been able to plow.

He grumped and glared around the house, sipping at his willow bark tea. "We could have had it plowed," he muttered, and Maria was not sure if he was mad that Poppy had gone lame, or mad that Pebblehoof had escaped.

Still, Poppy recovered just as Mr. Harper predicted. Bram's mood lightened with Poppy's recovery, and the mare was soon back to work.

"It is late, und we have missed some rain, but we will plow the rest anyway," Bram said. "No harm in trying. Maria, you will walk behind while I plow, und sow the wheat."

For the next five days, Maria walked slowly behind her father, the wet prairie soil clumping to her shoes. She tried to ignore the leaden weight of her muddy feet, and concentrated on letting a steady, measured stream of wheat kernels slip through her fingers onto the freshly turned soil.

With the wheat, she could keep up. Poppy wasn't so fast as Pebblehoof. But with the corn, and the need to mound up the soil into little hills, she fell far behind. It was two more days, with Bram helping, before the corn was in the ground. Stooping down soon put a pain in his back, and before long he took to crawling from one mound to the next, rather than take the bother of standing up.

Work on the farm picked up after that, and Maria's free afternoons became fewer and fewer. When they did come, she longed to go look for Pebblehoof, but held herself back. She wanted to give Pebblehoof time to forget what had happened, or at least time enough to forgive it.

Instead, she spent her afternoons weaving baskets. Laisa showed her different weaving patterns, ways to lay designs of squares and diamonds into a basket, and how to braid in a handle so it would never come loose.

Already they had a small stack of baskets in one corner of

the soddie, ones Laisa had decided were worthy enough to sell. "When we have enough, we will take them to Columbus," she said. The others, the ones with loose weaves or uneven shapes, they would use to put up stores for the winter.

Maria worked the garden, too. She hoed and watered, and weeded by hand around the smaller, more delicate plants.

Although working in the garden was not so agreeable as making baskets, she was glad to do it. She kept a careful eye on the carrots Laisa had planted early in the spring. She wished there was an apple tree anywhere on the homestead, but there was not. She knew horses loved apples, but there was nothing she could do about that. *Carrots will have to do*, she told herself.

At last, when Papa declared summer had finally come, the carrots were ready. Laisa began to take them from the garden, for stews and even to eat fresh. They were crunchy and sweet, and somehow held more juice than Maria would have imagined.

The next free afternoon she had, Maria asked, "May I pay a visit to Mr. Harper? I want to thank him again for Poppy."

"Ja," said Laisa. "Und invite him again for Sunday supper. It was nice having company."

Maria liked Mr. Harper. He was friendly, and had kept her secret. She would stop in to see him, of course, but that was not her true plan.

"And may I take some carrots? To eat on the walk back?"

Laisa gave Maria a curious look, but said, "Two only. Do not spoil your supper."

Maria smiled. "Thank you, Mama!" She dashed out to the garden. It was time to find Pebblehoof.

IT HAD BEEN weeks since Pebblehoof's escape. Maria had no idea where the herd might be, if it was even anywhere nearby. West along the wagon trail was as good a direction to start as any. The spring melt had passed and the rivers were lower now. She supposed, although she did not like to think about it, that the herd might have wandered far enough that she could never find them. Perhaps even into the Pawnee lands.

It was a hot and thirsty walk to Mr. Harper's, and Maria longed to bite into one of those juicy carrots. But she did not. She expected she would need them.

At length, she came into sight of Mr. Harper's cabin and found the man splitting shingles out by his wood pile.

"Afternoon, Mr. Harper," she called out.

Mr. Harper stuck his axe into the thick chopping block by his feet. He took a handkerchief from his shirt pocket, and wiped the sweat from his face.

"Afternoon, Miss Browning," he said. "I must say I'm a mite surprised to see you on two feet instead of four. How's that wild horse of yours?"

"I don't know," she said. "I haven't seen him since we finished plowing. Papa wanted to keep him, but he ran away soon as we had his collar off."

"Did you?"

"Want to keep him? Well, some," she admitted. "I do wish he was around all the time. But it didn't seem right. Pebblehoof isn't my horse, he's his own. And it seemed a downright dirty trick, after he saved our farm, to go and take him away from his herd and all."

Mr. Harper looked at her a long while, giving Maria the feeling he was reading her face. "You miss him, don't you?"

She nodded. "And I'm afraid if I ever do see him again, he'll just run away from me."

"Well now, that may be so. It may be. But maybe not. Horses are smart creatures. I reckon they understand more than they let on. You'll just have to wait and see."

Maria looked down at her feet. She hoped he was right. She hoped Pebblehoof knew it had been her father's idea, not hers. But she knew there was a danger in hoping, too. "I suppose it doesn't matter anyway. Papa told me I couldn't ride him anymore."

"That's hard, but I reckon your father knows best. Still, little miss," Mr. Harper went on, "what brings you by? You didn't walk all this way just to talk about horses."

"No, sir. I came to thank you again for fixing Poppy's hoof. She's all better now."

"Oh, that weren't nothing. Next time, your Pa'll know what to do."

"And to invite you again to Sunday supper," she added. "If you can come."

Mr. Harper smiled broad and wide. "Indeed I would! Your Ma sets a fine table, with company to match. This Sunday?"

Maria nodded. "Mm hmm."

"Good. It's settled, then." Mr. Harper took up the handle of the axe and worked the blade out of the chopping block. "I best carry on, miss. You have a good day, now."

Maria stood, wanting to go, but wanting to ask one more thing.

Mr. Harper set a fresh log up on the chopping block. "Something else on your mind?"

Maria swallowed. "Horses do like carrots, don't they?"

Mr. Harper glanced at the bulge in Maria's dress pocket, and the green fronds peeking out of it. He smiled.

"They do, Miss Browning. They do indeed. You tell your Ma I'll be pleased as punch to come to supper. I'll bring my fiddle all tuned up and ready to play."

"I will, sir. And thank you."

She turned and ran, unable to stop herself from hoping, out into the grass.

She made her way far into the prairie, searching, keeping one hand on the front of her dress so as not to lose her carrots.

She looked as long as she dared, keeping a careful eye on the sun's daily journey, but she did not find them. She turned for the homestead, and ate the carrots herself on the walk back.

Saturday came and went before Maria had another chance to go look, then Sunday came and her mother kept her at home to clean and help cook for company. True to his word, Mr. Harper brought his fiddle and they made a merry evening of it. Bram and Laisa even dared dance a turn around the table while Mr. Harper played.

Monday, Maria rose with her father to begin her chores early. She cleaned Poppy's stall and milked the cow and watered the garden and ran to the river for a fresh bundle of willow, scarcely stopping to breathe the whole time.

She finished her chores just before dinner, and when the midday meal was complete and the dishes scrubbed, she asked, "Mama, may I go out to look for wild onions?"

Laisa handed her a gathering basket. "It is early in the season, but ja. If you want to. They will be small now, so don't pull too many. Mark the spot, but leave the rest for now."

Maria pulled two more carrots on her way out, hoping her mother was not watching from the window. She had not asked, but it was only two.

This time she searched north. Before long, she found a wide path of pounded ground, just like they had left all around her that first day. *They galloped through here!*

She knelt down, touching her fingers to the earth. Impressed into the ground, she saw hoof prints. The marks were hard to make out, all jumbled atop one another. But the more she studied the markings, she began to see the pattern. The herd had been running east.

There was no new growth of grass, no tender green shoots poking up through the trampled stalks. She sprang up. The trail was still fresh, and she ran after them.

She ran a long way, again until the length of her shadow told her it was time to return, but she did not catch up to them. She returned with her basket, but without any onions.

She got away again the next day, and this time she headed straight for where she thought they would be. She found them, heads down in a hollow of green between two gentle hills.

Her heart raced at the sight of them. She wanted to run down the slope, to fly down to them, but dared not chance spooking them. She dropped down, hiding in the tall grass, peeking up just enough to look for Pebblehoof's white blaze.

When at last she saw it, she walked slowly towards the herd. She clicked her tongue and called his name. His head came up.

The herd shied away from her as she approached, and Pebblehoof moved with them.

"No, Pebblehoof. Don't run," she said, softly and to herself.

In a louder voice, she called to him. "It's all right, boy, I'm not going to take you back there. I just want to be friends again."

She kept up her words, walking step by step towards him. He slowed, allowing the rest of the herd to pass him by, until there was nothing between them but open space.

She reached into her pocket for the carrots which were still there from the day before, hoping they were still fresh enough.

"I brought you a treat." She held them out by their green tops, her arms outstretched. "Come on. Horses like carrots. I know you've never tried any, but they're good."

Pebblehoof did not approach her, but neither did he back away as she came to him. At last, the carrots were close enough for him to bite them, but still he did not.

"It's all right, really," she said. "Look." While Pebblehoof watched, she lifted one of the carrots to her mouth and snapped off a bite. It wasn't quite so fresh anymore, but it was still good.

She held them out to him again. He nipped with his lips. She let go as he pulled the root into his mouth and crunched it up.

"There, see?" she said. She took one small step backwards, tempting him forward with the other carrot. He stepped and took it.

She dared reach up him, stroking his velvety nose and smooth, strong neck. "Good boy." She laid her cheek on him. "I'm so happy to see you."

Pebblehoof snuffled at her, and in moments she was on his back just like before.

She clicked and urged him into a run, the familiar exhilaration rising up to fill her stomach, her chest, her throat until she burst out in laughter.

She let Pebblehoof run free, not caring where they went. They rode far and fast, curving a wide arc across the landscape. They passed near enough to see the buildings of Columbus across the Loup River valley, before bending around toward the homestead.

The high summer sun was on Maria's face as they rode back, Pebblehoof still at a run and showing no signs of tiring. Maria settled into the easy rhythm of Pebblehoof's stride. *I could ride like this forever.*

They reached the wagon trail and followed it. Up ahead, Maria saw a familiar dark line crossing the trail. A memory of tumbling, falling, came to mind.

She leaned back a notch. "Whoa up, boy," she said. "Let's slow down."

Pebblehoof did not slow down, and the stream came closer. She leaned further back. "Slow down, please!" She remembered the pain of crashing to the ground and the desperate, drowning feeling of having the wind knocked out of her. Not knowing what to do, she reached for his mane and pulled.

At last, Pebblehoof slowed. His gallop broke to a trot, then a walk.

"Good boy." When they reached the stream, Maria slid off, her heart pounding. She fell to her knees on the bank, scooping handfuls of cold water to drink. Pebblehoof dropped his head to drink with her.

When her heart had slowed and her thirst was quenched, she stood. "Thank you for the ride," she said, "but I'll walk home from here. You get on back to your herd, now."

CHAPTER 14

THE NEXT MORNING, Bram handed Maria a shovel and announced, "Today, you will help me dig the root cellar. Klarina, you do Maria's chores today."

Klarina groaned. "Do I have to?"

"Don't talk back, Kleine Maus," he said. "You must learn to do these things eventually."

"Do I have to fill the wood box, too?"

Bram nodded. "You are strong enough now. Go on."

Klarina grumbled off to the wood pile, and Bram led Maria outside, to a part of the wall near where the kitchen was.

"We will dig here, und later make a door to the inside. No more fighting through the snow in the winter to get to the storage pit, ja?"

Maria smiled. She well remembered the chore of going outside in the dead of winter, digging with frozen hands to get at the carrots and potatoes stored in pits lined with hay and covered with soil. Having a real root cellar with a door into the house would be heaven.

"And it will save wood, won't it?" she asked. Not having to open the front door would keep the house warmer, too.

Bram smiled at her and nodded. He paced around that side of the house, then ran back inside to check a measurement. When he returned, he motioned with his shovel. "About here, you think?"

Maria was surprised he would ask, but yes, the place he indicated looked about right. "Yes, Papa. How big do we make it?"

Bram pulled at his beard. "Better too big than too small, I think."

He used his shovel to mark out a rectangle about five feet wide, and extending outward from the side of the house. Maria gulped. It would be a big hole, when they were finished.

"How deep do we have to make it?" she asked.

"As deep as the house." The Brownings' soddie was dug a good three feet into the prairie, about up to Bram's waist. "We will cut the sod out first und make walls. Then we will dig out, und if we need, take more sod from the fields to finish."

When Bram was satisfied with the outline he had marked out, he showed Maria how to cut the sod with her shovel.

It was hard work, forcing the shovel blade down through the tough mat of roots that made up the sod. It was hard to keep the cuts straight and even. They made large bricks a foot wide and two feet long. Bram cut three bricks to Maria's one, but he did not chide her for being slow.

Sweat dripped down Maria's forehead and off the tip of her nose, even though it was only morning and the sun was not yet high. Her hands began to tingle with the warning of blisters before the cutting was half done.

Still, she thought, *it's nice, working with Papa.* In Chicago, she would never have had such a chance, with him always off at the print shop, and her in school or watching Klarina while her mother was at the textile mill.

It felt good to be old enough to help with the work, too. She was pleased and proud, though she would not say so out loud, to help with a job that would make the coming winter that much more bearable.

After a time, she asked, "Papa, might I work in the print shop with you someday?"

Bram stopped, his shovel sticking up out of the ground. He looked at her, his face full of surprise. "You want to learn printing?"

"Maybe. I don't know what it's like. But I'd like to try."

Bram dabbed his forehead with a handkerchief, but when he lifted his head it was not to answer her. He was looking at something over her shoulder.

She turned, and saw a familiar-looking man approaching on a horse. Not Mr. Harper, but someone else. A man in a wide-brimmed hat. *That railroad man*, she thought.

The man rode slow and easy, until he was close enough to wave and shout out "Hallo, Brownings!"

"Papa, it's that Mr. Seymour, isn't it?"

"Ja, I believe so," Bram said. He walked out to meet the man by the paddock fence, where the man had stopped to tie his horse. Maria followed.

Seymour tipped his hat to Maria, and Bram shook the man's hand.

"Mr. Seymour," Bram said, "I did not expect you to come out again."

"Well, sir, I have news. I've come to clear up this business about the lay of the railroad line."

"Ja? Gut. So, you will go around my markers, then?"

"Well, Mr. Browning, I wouldn't say that, exactly."

Bram folded his arms. "What would you say, exactly?"

"Well, sir, by the survey I made this past April, I make your northwest boundary marker at two thousand, five hundred and eighty feet from the river. The rail bed, however, shall lie one thousand and three hundred feet from the river."

"But that will cross my land! You promised you would not cross my land." Bram's voice was raised, and Maria could make out the hard line of his jaw under his dark brown beard.

"No sir, I made no such promise," said Mr. Seymour. "Perhaps you misunderstood. I gather English is not your first language."

"Nein!" Bram shouted. "I understood you perfectly. You said you would take us into account. Those were your words, Seymour."

"And I did take you into account." Now Mr. Seymour's arms were crossed as well. "Nevertheless, the line shall run one thousand and three hundred feet from the river."

Bram swore something in German. He shifted in his spot, looking from the house to the boundary markers in the distance. His eyes blazed. "That will run straight through my house!"

"That is correct, Mr. Browning. Your house, unfortunately, must be demolished. You and your family will have to move."

"Nonsense!" Bram's hands were at his sides now, his fists clenched. "This is *my* land. I have marked and filed my claim, exactly to the requirements of the Homestead Act. You have no right, und I will not allow this."

"There, I'm afraid you're wrong, sir," Mr. Seymour said. "This isn't your land."

"What? Ridiculous! I live here. I work this land, just as is written in the Act. It is mine, I tell you."

"Not yet, it isn't. It's still the government's land. And the

Union Pacific Railroad, Mr. Browning, is under contract to that United States Government to build a railroad. I, in turn, am in the employ of the Union Pacific Railroad to build that railroad from Columbus, westward, at the location I judge most efficacious."

"I know what the Homestead Act says," Bram shot back. "I set the text of it myself for the paper in Chicago. I know every word of it, und it says I may stake my claim and make it mine. It says nothing about railroads."

"But it does say the land will only be yours after five years, Mr. Browning. I've reviewed all the claims on this stretch of river at the land office in Omaha. You haven't been here but a little over a year, now. You'll have to stay four more to make it yours, but by then the railroad will be finished. Right now, this land is more mine than yours, and I'm saying you need to move."

Laisa and Klarina stood at the soddie's door, watching. Maria felt a sinking queasiness in her stomach. *Why won't he just go away?* She wished he had never come at all.

"You are the one who needs to move, Mr. Seymour. Right now." Maria saw the tremble in her father's fists, held stiffly at his sides.

But Mr. Seymour did not budge.

Bram roared. His hands shot forward, shoving Mr. Seymour in the chest. "Out, Teufelsmensch! Go!"

Mr. Seymour staggered backwards, barely staying upright. Bram marched ahead, pushing and shoving the man towards his horse.

"I will go over your head," Bram yelled. "I will do what I must, but I have worked too hard here. I'll be damned if I let go even one tenth of one acre to you." He kicked at Mr. Seymour's shins as the man scrambled up into his saddle.

Bram yanked loose the hitch knot on the rope to Seymour's horse. Mr. Seymour backed his horse away from the paddock fence and away from Bram. He glared at Bram with venom in his eyes. "You're right about that, Mr. Browning. You just might be." He pivoted his horse around and rode off at a gallop.

Bram stood, watching Mr. Seymour shrink into the distance. His chest heaved and his face was bright red.

Maria asked, "You just might be what, Papa?" But Bram gave no answer.

CHAPTER 15

MARIA COULDN'T SHAKE the sick feeling in her gut all that afternoon while she and Bram finished cutting and stacking the thick sod slabs into walls. She couldn't shake it that evening, as she helped Laisa prepare dinner, nor even as she lay down to sleep.

At breakfast, she finally dared voice her question. "Papa, will we really have to leave?"

She supposed she wouldn't miss the soddie too much, with its earthen walls always dropping crumbs of dirt onto her bed and into her hair. She wouldn't miss some of the harder chores. *But,* she thought, *I'd miss Pebblehoof.*

Bram gave her a smile like watered milk. "Do not worry, Schatzie. Mr. Seymour must be wrong. He cannot do this thing."

"But he said—"

Bram held up a hand for silence. "I know what he said, but it cannot be correct. I will go to Columbus today. Even Mr. Seymour must have a boss, ja? I will find this man, und sort everything out."

Bram ate quickly while Laisa packed him a sack dinner. He took his rifle, and off he went.

Laisa clapped her hands together. "Come, girls. Today will be a busy day. Maria, you finish your chores, then we must do laundry."

Maria's shoulders sagged. *Not laundry.* It would take up the whole afternoon, and if they were going to have to move, she wanted as much time with Pebblehoof as she could get.

"Do not grumble," Laisa said. "Your clothes are filthy after digging yesterday."

Maria milked the cow. She let Poppy out into the paddock to walk around while she cleaned the stall and spread fresh hay. She filled the wood box and used the small hatchet—Bram said she was too small to try the big axe yet—to split a few pieces of firewood into kindling.

Laisa served a quick dinner, then handed Maria a bucket. "I'll get the wash tub. You bring the water. Klarina, you fetch out the soap pot."

Laisa hauled the two big, tin wash tubs out into the front yard. Maria pulled up pails of water from the well to fill the tubs while Laisa brought out the clothes. Klarina handed her mother the brown earthenware soap pot.

"Kleine Maus, can you fetch the washboards too?"

Klarina nodded and ran back inside.

Laisa scooped a handful of soft soap out of the pot and mixed it into the water. She peeked into the pot. "Ach. Almost out. We will have to make soap soon."

"Can I help this time?" Maria asked. Soap making was like magic, the way the lye and the fat drippings Laisa had been saving all year somehow turned into soap. They hadn't made soap since before winter had come, and then, Maria hadn't been allowed to help on account of the lye. "I know to be careful."

"Ja," Laisa said. "I think perhaps this year, we mix in some herbs. What do you think? Give the soap a nice smell."

Maria nodded. "Or maybe some flowers. There's some nice smelling ones down by the river."

Klarina returned with two washboards. Laisa and Maria took up their stations at either end of the tub and set to work.

One by one, trousers, shirts, and dresses sank into the water to be rubbed up and down on the washboard ridges. They handed wet, soapy clothes to Klarina, who rinsed them in the second tub, then spread them out to dry on tufts of prairie grass.

The wash water turned brown with dirt, the rinse water bubbled with soap, and both had to be changed.

"I hope we do not have to leave," Laisa remarked. "Laundry here is much better than in the tenement. You remember, Schatzie?"

Maria nodded. In Chicago, she had to fetch buckets of water up and down the stairs from the tenement house's pump on the ground floor, and they had to hang the wet clothes on lines strung across their parlor. The clothes took days to dry, and gave the rooms a dank, moist smell.

Here, the well was just a few feet away. It was easy to dump the dirty water out in the grass. And the clothes, laid out in the summer sun, would be dry before suppertime.

They finished the washing and folded what was already dry. Maria found she had an hour or so to herself before the rest would be ready to fold. *Not enough time,* she thought, as she gazed out into the wilds.

She walked out to the fields to look at the corn and wheat. She sat down in the warm grass, watching grasshoppers climb and jump among the stalks. Lazy clouds drifted across the big sky.

Bram came home as Maria was putting away the last of the

folded clothes. He hung his rifle on its pegs and handed Laisa a fat prairie chicken he had shot on the walk home. She gave him his cup of willow bark tea, which he cradled in his hands but did not drink.

Her father wore a blank look, the one Maria knew meant he was mad inside.

"Well?" Laisa asked.

Bram sighed deeply and eased himself down at the table. "I do not know. Mr. Seymour, he is the head man for the railroad in Columbus. I would go over his head, only I do not know where to go or who to talk to."

"Did you talk to Seymour, then?"

Bram shook his head. "Nein. After yesterday... I know. I should not have struck him."

"Nein," said Laisa, and it was all she said.

Bram slapped the table top with the flat of his hand. "Still. We will do something. I will not be driven like a beggar from the bakery door! This is our land, and we are not leaving."

A WEEK PASSED. Maria managed to get away from farm work twice. Once, she rode the wagon trail as far as the Loup river, and saw where the railroad workers were setting piles for a bridge. The other time, she went west, past Mr. Harper's, and on a long ways until she found another homestead.

Out front was a Conestoga, its wooden hoops and canvas cover standing up straight and bright in the sunshine. A man and a woman were carrying boxes and furnishings from the house into the wagon.

Maria waved when she was close enough, and the couple waved back. She rode up.

"Good day to you." Maria introduced herself and said she lived a few miles up the trail.

The man said, "Ah. I think I met your father in Columbus, once. You may give him the regards of Mr. and Mrs. Carter, but I'm afraid we're not likely to meet again."

"You're leaving?" Maria asked.

"Well, yes," said Mr. Carter. "Have to. The railroad, you know."

"But what will you do?" Maria asked.

"Oh, my wife's got kin down to Fort Kearny. We'll help work their land and stay the winter. Next spring we'll start somewhere new. Besides, it'll be good to be by the fort. My wife gets nervous, being so close to Pawnee land. 'Course I see you riding Indian style. Maybe that don't bother you so much."

Maria wasn't sure what to say to that. As far as she knew, the Pawnee didn't make trouble for anybody.

"What about you?" Mr. Carter asked. "Aren't you leaving?"

"I don't know. My papa says no, but I don't know what's going to happen."

The man shook his head. "You tell your pa not to be so stubborn. Can't fight the railroad."

Mr. Carter tipped his hat as Maria rode off. It was late, and she needed to get home. She thought about what he had said the whole way, and whether to tell her parents about it.

But if she did, they would know she was still riding Pebblehoof, and she'd catch a mess of trouble for sure. *And they wouldn't like that I rode so far, either*, she thought. So when she returned she kept quiet. There wouldn't be any use in getting Bram all riled up.

Maria walked past the four acres, as they had taken to calling them, on the way in. The corn was up past her knees now, and the wheat was growing well too. But on the other sixteen acres the plants were much smaller.

She saw a horse, not Poppy, tied at the paddock fence. Its nose was down in a bucket of water. For a moment she thought it might be Mr. Seymour, back to have it out with Bram, and she ran towards the house. But as she approached, she could see it was a different horse.

When she entered, Reverend Tinney was there.

"Wash up, Maria," said Laisa. "We have company for supper. "You will stay to supper, won't you, Reverend?"

Tinney smiled. He and Bram were seated at the table. "That I will, and gladly. In my line of work, a man never knows when he'll see a home-cooked meal."

The reverend turned back to Bram. "I see you plowed quite a field since I was last through."

"Ja," said Bram. "But we had some trouble with our horse. She was lame for a spell, and most of it was plowed late."

Tinney shook his head. "That is most unfortunate. The Lord does test us."

Maria rubbed a wet cloth over her hands and face, and sat quietly with Klarina on their bed to wait for supper. Bram shrugged. "Even if it does not ripen, it will make ample silage for the winter."

"True. In every misfortune may be found a blessing, if you look for it. Still, things will turn up, I'm certain. You'll have your orchard soon, and with the railroad coming through—"

"Ach! Do not talk of the railroad," Bram said. His lips twisted in a sneer.

"Why ever not?" Tinney asked.

Bram told the whole story from the beginning, then asked, "But I do not know what to do, Reverend. What do you think?"

The reverend stroked the black leather cover of his small Bible. "Well, I'm a man of God, so won't say as I know the law of it, as to who has the stronger claim on the land. But I agree it doesn't

seem right they could force you good folks out. What about that
Mr. Dodge you mentioned? The one who made the first survey."

"What about him?" Bram asked.

"Well, I've heard his name often enough between here and
Omaha. I believe he's the chief engineer for the Union Pacific. If
you don't like this Mr. Seymour's plan, seems you ought to take
it up with him."

"Mr. Seymour seemed most certain it was his survey that
mattered."

"That may be," Tinney said. "I couldn't say. But it might also
be that Mr. Seymour's making more of himself than he really
is. And who's to say otherwise? No, you need to find this Mr.
Dodge. Make certain he knows what's happening. Like as not, he
only knows what Seymour tells him anyway."

Bram pulled at his beard and nodded. Then he slapped his
hand on the table. "By Gott, I will do it."

"That's right. A man's work ought to be sacred, you ask me.
And I don't know anybody that works harder than you homesteaders. Pray with me, Mr. Browning. Let us ask God's blessing
on your land, and that all will turn out for the best."

Tinney bowed his head and prayed. Maria was surprised to
see her father join in, even though Reverend Tinney was a Baptist.

After the amens, Tinney said, "You know who else you might
have a word with?"

"Who?" Bram asked.

"George Train. He's the big man in Columbus, isn't that right?
He has a lot of land up there, but as far as I know he has no stake in
the railroad. If anybody'll know what you might do, it'll be him."

Bram agreed to make another trip to Columbus, as soon as he
could manage, to find George Train and inquire after Mr. Dodge.
"Und I will plant my orchard this fall," he said.

"So soon?" Tinney asked.

Bram waved the question away. "This is my land. There is nothing on this earth that will make me leave, railroad or no, so I will plant. I will not lose a whole year over wondering."

Bram's mood eased considerably with the prospect of not one possible ally, but two, and they spent an agreeable evening with Reverend Tinney.

CHAPTER 16

BRAM SET OUT the next morning to mark places for the trees in his orchard and to begin cutting the sod out where each would be planted. It was another two weeks before he was ready to go to Columbus.

In that time, Maria had the chore of digging out the rest of the root cellar, and banking the soil against the cellar's sod walls. The thicker the walls, Bram explained, the better their larder would keep.

The digging was enjoyable, after a fashion. The soil was soft, and at the end of the day she could mark her work by standing in a place that had not existed before.

But when the digging was done, she was again free to mind herself. She rode Pebblehoof once more down the wagon trail to the Carter's homestead. The whole place was quiet. They had taken everything with them, even the window glass out of the frames.

"Hallo!" Maria called out, but no one answered. She rode Pebblehoof slowly around the abandoned soddie, and rested a few minutes in the building's cool interior while Pebblehoof munched grass in the yard.

The empty house, stripped bare and breezy through the empty windows, gave her an uneasy feeling. She stepped outside again soon. She picked a few carrots from the Carter's front garden, ones that had been too small for the couple to have bothered to take with them, and gave them to Pebblehoof.

"I hope they made it to Fort Kearny all right," she said, as she mounted up. "Come on, boy. I don't like it here." She rode back that afternoon in a quiet, sober mood.

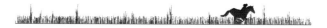

THEN CAME THE morning Bram announced, "Maria. Gather up some baskets. We are going to Columbus."

Maria jumped up. "Can I, really?"

"Ja," Bram nodded. "We need some things from LeClerc's, und it a good chance to see if he will approve of your baskets. Also, I will try again to talk to Mr. Seymour."

Maria beamed. Her mother said, "Let me help pick the best ones."

Laisa sorted through the stack of baskets in one corner of the house, a stack that had grown nearly as tall as Maria with the combined efforts of all three of them.

Laisa separated the stack into two piles. One to sell, and one to keep. All of Laisa's baskets went into the sell pile. They were beautiful, with smooth curves, straight sides, and perfectly tight, even weaving all around.

Maria was pleased that more than half of her own baskets went into the sell pile too.

At last, Laisa came to a final basket and stopped. She turned to Maria. "Who made this one? Was it you or me?"

Maria examined a small basket, finely made from the thinnest willow. "That was mine. I made it last week."

Laisa smiled and gave her a hug. "This is fine work, Schatzie. You are as good as me, now."

Bram looped a rope around the basket handles and carried them outside while Maria and Laisa packed food for the trip. Maria changed into her Sunday best clothes.

When she came outside, Bram had Poppy's saddle and bridle on her, and had arranged the bundle of baskets across Poppy's back, hanging down half on each side.

"Come, then," said Bram. "It is a long walk we must make."

"Can't we ride?" Maria asked.

"Nein. I would not hurt Poppy's hoof again."

The walk was long indeed. Maria wished she could just call for Pebblehoof and have him appear. How much nicer it would be to ride, and faster too. She struggled to keep up with her father's long strides, and did not complain.

They walked in silence for a long ways. A question weighed on Maria's mind. "Papa, are we really going to have to move?" *And if we do*, she wondered, *wherever will we end up?*

"I do not know," he said. "But I have been thinking. Perhaps this is a good thing. The railroad has money from the government. If they will buy out my claim, we may move to Columbus this year. Open my print shop right away, ja?"

Maria's face lit up. *And I wouldn't have to leave Pebblehoof!* "Really, Papa? Do you think so?"

"If they will give me a fair price. Why not?" He put a hand around her shoulder as they walked, and gave her a squeeze.

At last, they reached the Loup River. Maria's back was hot with the sun, her front moist with sweat under her dress. It was high summer and the river was low. But even so, Bram lifted Maria up and set her in the saddle on Poppy's back, just in front of the bundle of baskets.

"Let Poppy carry you across," he said, "und we will eat while we dry off."

Maria felt wrong to be sitting in a hard leather saddle rather than riding bareback. The thick saddle hid the shift and roll of Poppy's muscles from her, and she felt as though Poppy were far away from her as Bram led them both across the river.

Even at its low summer ebb, the river came midway up Bram's chest at the deepest part. The cool water gave ease to her tired feet as they dangled in.

Once across, they ate while drying in the sun and watching the workers building the railroad bridge a little ways downstream.

Bram hopped up and brushed dust and crumbs from his hands. He was not fully dry, but close enough. "Come. We have much to do."

Maria's excitement grew as they climbed the river banks up to the town above. She had not been to Columbus since spring of the previous year, on the family's trip west. She remembered how tiny it had seemed, compared to Chicago.

And it was tiny. Just a handful of buildings, alone on the plain. Still it was more humanity than Maria had seen in a long time and her heart raced with more than just the effort of walking.

Maria stayed close to her father as they made their way into town. He stopped in front of a wooden building and tied Poppy's lead rope to the hitching post out front. Maria read the sign above the door, carefully sounding out the words. "LeClerc's Dry Goods and Trading Post."

"Ja, gut," Bram said. He removed the baskets and carried them into the store.

The store was a bewildering jumble of everything. Barrels were clustered all over, full of wheat, beans, corn, nails, flour, and the butt-ends of new, white axe handles. Tools of every kind lined the walls and hung from the ceiling. Bolts of cloth in denim, canvas, and fine colorful calicos lay stacked behind a long wooden counter, and next to those a rack on the wall held every color thread she could possibly imagine, all on perfectly even, round spools.

Maria scarcely knew where to look first.

The shopkeeper saw them enter, and called out, "Bonjour, M'sieu Browning! And who is zees you 'ave brought with you today?"

Bram came forward, leading Maria by the hand, and introduced her to Mr. LeClerc. He was a barrel-chested man, dressed in store-bought clothes with an apron over his outfit. His face was shaved, showing just enough stubble for Maria to see his beard would be white if he let it grow.

Mr. LeClerc came out from behind the long wooden counter to shake her hand. "Et bonjour, Maria. I am delight to see such a jolie fille in my shop."

Maria had to strain her ears to make out the man's accent, and half what he said she couldn't understand.

"My daughter has some business with you, Mr. LeClerc." Bram handed Maria the roped bundle of baskets. "Go on, Schatzie."

Maria looked at her father, her forehead crinkled up. "Papa, I thought—"

"Nein," Bram said, his hand held up flat. "They are your work. It is your business." He turned his back and wandered over to look at some tools.

Maria's head spun. She had never done business with anyone before. "Well, sir," she began, "I want to sell you these baskets. My mama and I—I mean, my mother and I—we made them."

Mr. LeClerc eyed the baskets and stroked his fingers up and

down his jaw, rasping against his stubble.

"They're willow," Maria added. *How much should I ask?* Laisa hadn't said anything about the price.

Mr. LeClerc untied one of the big baskets, the bushel-sized ones, from the rope. He squeezed and pulled at it, testing the strength.

A memory came to her, unbidden, from Chicago. She remembered being in a shop and how Laisa had warned her not to touch anything.

"If you break it, I'll have to charge you," she said.

Mr. LeClerc's hands froze, but his eyes held laughter. "Ah, someone 'as taught you well, n'est-ce pas?" He handed the basket to her. "Bon! Ils sont tres forte. What will you take for zem, eh?"

Maria swallowed hard and guessed. "Ten cents each?"

"Vraiment?" he asked. He gave her a sideways look and held up ten fingers. "Ten? Do I 'ear you correctly?"

Maria nodded, wondering if she had asked too much. She was about to suggest five cents each when he spoke.

"Ah! No, no, it ees not good." He crossed his hands quickly back and forth in front of him.

"Five cents?"

"No, arrête! Stop. You would have me rob you, eh? You are lucky Remy LeClerc ees an honest man. Allez!"

He motioned her over to another corner of the store, where other baskets lay in neat stacks by size.

"Cinq cents! If I buy for zees only, I cannot sleep at night. Look." He pointed to the big bushel baskets. "Zees ones, good for holding maize, pommes — potatoes, eh? — fifty cents." He went down the line, size by size, telling Maria the prices of each.

When he was done, he said, "Maintenent. We start again, eh? I also must earn a living, so again, what will you take for your baskets?"

It took a while to haggle each one out, but one by one they came to agreement. Mr. LeClerc wrote the figures on a slip of paper, tallied them up, and showed her.

"So. We say five dollars forty cents toutes ensemble?"

Maria's eyes boggled. *Five whole dollars?* She looked carefully at the line of numbers, struggling to recollect how her mother had taught her to do sums. But it was more numbers than she had ever added together before, and she couldn't keep them straight in her head.

Finally, she said, "Papa? Will you check the sum?"

Bram nodded and came over. He looked at the slip of paper for a long minute, then said, "Ja. It is correct. Danke, Mr. LeClerc."

Mr. LeClerc held out his hand and Maria shook it. He counted out coins from the till into a pile.

When he was done, he slid the coins across the counter to her. She scooped them into her hands and took them to her father. "Here, Papa."

But Bram shook his head. "It is not all mine," he said. "How much is from your baskets?"

Maria's jaw dropped. "You mean I can keep some?"

Bram nodded. "It is from your work. What do you think is fair?"

Maria thought. More of the baskets, and especially the larger ones, had been her mother's work. Still, many had been hers.

"Maybe two dollars."

Bram waited while Maria counted out three fifty cent pieces and five dimes, then gave him the rest.

"What will you do with your money?" he asked.

"I don't know." Maria had never had money, let alone two dollars. She walked around the store, clutching the cool silver coins until they grew warm in her hand.

She thought about shoes, or cloth to make dresses. She thought about hard candy, which she sometimes had in Chicago on her birthday or Christmas. She thought about Klarina, whose birthday was coming in the fall, and about her father and his print shop.

While she wandered the store, Bram bought a sack of nails, a new hammer and saw, a two-handled draw knife, a cake of dark reddish rosin, and a pound bag of sugar.

At last, Maria settled on two things. For three dimes, she bought a real cloth doll with a beautiful painted china face for Klarina's birthday. And with the nickel she got in change, she bought a small sack of lemon-flavored hard candy.

The rest she held out to Bram as they stepped out of the store.

"Schatzie, nein," he said. "It is yours."

"Yes, Papa," she said. This, she decided, was how she could help her father with his dream. "And I want you to keep it for your shop."

She put the coins into his cupped hand. Bram held the coins, looking at them. At last he put them in his pocket, where they clinked against the rest. "Meine leibe Maria," he said, and he kissed the top of her head.

He was silent while he packed their purchases carefully into Poppy's saddlebags, then said, "Come. Now we will see about this railroad, ja?"

MARIA STOOD OUTSIDE the railroad office with Poppy while Bram went inside. The steady beat of the blacksmith's hammer rang out from the smithy across the street. The hammer stopped, and Maria watched a young man pump a bellows while an older man stuck a work piece back into the fire. It came out again a minute later, a glowing white stick of iron, and the hammer rang out again.

Between hammer blows, Maria heard raised voices from inside the railroad office. A minute later, the door swung open and Bram came back out.

"Was Mr. Dodge there, Papa?"

Bram flicked a hand in front of his face. "Nein. Only that same boy from before, und still he has no manners. I had half a mind to give him a good thrashing."

"You didn't!"

"Of course not. He said I must only talk to Mr. Seymour, where they are making the depot. Come. I know what I will say to him."

Maria held Poppy's lead rope and followed her father off the main street, to a place that was a hive of activity. At least a dozen men were hard at work. Masons chiseled large stones square while others dry-fitted them into a foundation. Lumbermen straddled over round logs, hewing flats onto two sides, their adzes flashing in the sun.

Maria spied Mr. Seymour's familiar wide-brimmed hat on the other side, and pointed to him. Bram cupped his hands around his mouth. "Mr. Seymour," he called. His voice boomed out, and for a moment, every head turned to look at them.

Mr. Seymour made his way over. "Mr. Browning, how good to see you again. What brings you out to the depot?"

"I have decided. I will move—"

Mr. Seymour interrupted. "You will? That's excellent. I knew you were a smart man, sir."

"I am not finished," Bram continued. He crossed his arms in front of himself. "I will move, if the railroad will buy out my claim."

Mr. Seymour's arms also crossed. "I see. And what price would you be asking for your claim?"

Maria looked at the two men. *Except for Mr. Seymour's hat and Papa's beard*, Maria thought, *there might as well be a mirror between them.*

"Your new line takes half my land. Mr. Dodge offered me ten dollars to the acre. You can have the rest for five to the acre. Plus an allowance for improvements. One thousand four hundred dollars."

Mr. Seymour's eyes went wide. Then he laughed, loud and hard. "Fourteen hundred dollars? Is that right, or are there bees in my ears?"

"It is only fair, you will agree."

"Fair? Fair? It's outrageous!" He hollered to his men, "Listen to this, boys. This here German fellow wants fourteen hundred United States dollars for his claim and his sad little soddie shack. What do you think of that?"

A few of the men laughed. Others shook their heads and looked away. Mr. Seymour jerked his thumb towards his workers. "Even they know that's ridiculous."

Bram set his jaw. "You insult my home? It is a fair price. I will not haggle it with you."

"I'm not going to buy your claim, Mr. Browning. Not for fourteen hundred dollars, not for fourteen cents. And I won't haggle *that* with you!"

"Nein? Then I will have your guarantee, sir," Bram said.

"Guarantee, Mr. Browning? And what guarantee might that be?"

"If you will not buy me out, then I will not move. You will sign a paper saying that your railroad will not cross my land."

Mr. Seymour snorted. "I'll sign no such thing. I believe I made my position clear before. Go away, Mr. Browning. I have important matters to attend to."

Bram raised his voice. "You will give me your guarantee, or I will have it from Mr. Dodge."

Seymour's eyebrows raised up a notch. "Well, someone's

been talking to you. Now that is funny."

"What?" Bram asked. "What is funny?"

"You, going to go see Mr. Dodge, that's what. Not likely, sir. Grenville Dodge is in the far west to settle a route through the Rocky Mountains. What will you do? Head out to find him? Leave your family all alone for weeks or months? Leave your land untended while summer passes? Or pack 'em up in your wagon and take them with you?"

A wicked smile broke out on Mr. Seymour's face, and he went on. "Why, yes. Perhaps you ought to do that very thing. That would suit me fine. Clear out, then. Go get your paper signed. By the time you get back the railroad will be right where I said it would be."

Bram's fists tightened while he listened. When Mr. Seymour stopped, his arms were straight stiff at his sides again. When he spoke, his voice was low and slow. "I will have your—"

Maria saw Mr. Seymour flick his eyes down to Bram's fists. "No sir. No guarantee. Now get out."

Bram growled from somewhere deep in his throat. His fist jerked back to strike. Maria gasped, but Bram held his fist, poised there by his shoulder.

Mr. Seymour flinched.

Everyone in the work yard was looking again. Bram shouted, "This is not over. I will never leave! It is not over, you hear?"

He snatched Poppy's lead rope from Maria's hand, and marched away. Maria ran to catch up with him.

Mr. Seymour called after them, "You got that right, you hard-headed Hessian!"

Bram spun on his heel, fists clenched again.

"No, Papa," Maria said, but her voice was small.

"What did you call me?" Bram said.

"You heard me, Fritz." Mr. Seymour spat on the ground at Bram's feet. "Now get out of my depot, unless you'd rather I call my men over."

Bram glared. "Please, Papa," Maria said. "I want to go home."

Without a word, Bram turned away from the depot again.

"While you're at it, get out of Platte County!" Seymour yelled as they stepped into the street. Maria gripped her father's arm, not looking back. Bram didn't either.

Neither of them spoke a word as they marched back through town. At the Loup River, Bram silently swooped Maria up onto Poppy's back for the crossing. Only much later, after they had risen out of the river valley and up onto the high prairie, after Bram's pace had slowed to a walk and his shoes no longer squished with river water on each step, did either of them break the silence.

"You tried, Papa. It sounded like a fair price to me."

"If only I could take an audience with this Mr. Dodge," he said, "I am sure he would listen."

Maria did not answer. They still had a very long walk ahead of them.

CHAPTER 17

WHEN MARIA AWOKE the next morning, Bram was not there. Laisa said he had taken his axe and gone down to the river to fell trees, and that Maria was to join him.

"Eat your breakfast, Schatzie, und go help. Klarina can do your chores today."

Maria ate, then followed the sound of the axe. She made her way into the trees covering the bottom land until she found her father.

"Ah, Maria," Bram said, when she arrived. "Gut." She watched, while he cut through the last of a small tree. Five more powerful blows, and they watched it fall. When it was down, he severed the splintered end from the stump with a final chop, and pointed to a small pile of similar logs nearby. A hatchet lay across the pile.

"Cut the branches from the trees, und drag them up to the house," he told her.

"Yes, Papa." Maria picked up the hatchet, its smooth handle and heavy steel blade familiar in her hand from chopping kindling wood. "What are they for?"

"The root cellar. We must line it with logs to keep it dry und keep animals from digging through. Und also for the roof."

Bram showed her how to bend the green branches forward and tap them with the hatchet blade so the wood snapped open where each branch met the tree trunk. One by one, she clipped them off while Bram selected another tree and began to chop.

Her log was small and she could just fit her two hands around it, fingers to fingers and thumb to thumb. The few logs Bram had already cut were the same, and they were all very long, too. From the fat ends to their skinny tips, she could see they would be much longer than needed to reach the top of the root cellar.

"Papa, should I cut them shorter?" she asked.

"Nein. We will cut them later, after they are in place. Take it to the house now."

Maria reached two arms under the log she had just stripped. She strained to lift it. It shifted, then tottered to one side. She moved her balance and tried again, but it was too heavy.

"I can't do it," she said.

"Do not lift," Bram said between axe blows. "Pull it."

Maria held it by the skinny end, and heaved backwards. Sure enough, the log moved. Just a few inches, but it moved. *I did it!* She pulled and pulled, making more distance with each effort as she found her stride.

Still, it was murderous work, navigating the log through the maze of trees in the bottom land. The humid river air stifled her, and sweat slicked her all over. Once out of the trees, it was better. The breeze reached her, and on the open grass she could manage a slow but steady walk.

Her legs burned with each step forward, but at last she reached the house and laid the log next to the root cellar.

Bram had finished the root cellar's walls with sod cut from the fields, all except a space at the end so they could get into it to work. The cellar now stood as high as the house above ground, and as deep below ground to match. But its roof was still open to the sky, and its sides an undressed mess of dirt and roots.

Maria sat for a minute in the cool underground of the root cellar, shaded by its high walls, to catch her breath.

The day passed this way. Trim a log. Pull it back to the house. Over and over. Even working as fast as she could, she could not keep up with Bram's axe. After the fifth log, when blisters were stinging on her palms, Maria asked, "How many do we need?"

"I think one hundred," Bram said. "If it is too many, we will use them for firewood."

Inside, Maria groaned. *One hundred logs?* It was hard even to imagine how big a pile that would be. She trimmed a branch from the next log. "Why can't Poppy pull them?" she asked.

"The ground is too rough. Too many stumps, und hollow places. I do not want her to hurt a hoof again."

Pebblehoof could do it, she thought and she longed to go look for him. Pebblehoof could pull ten logs all at once, she was sure. But she dared not mention it. She knew the only reason her punishment had not been worse last time was because Pebblehoof had plowed for them. That wouldn't work this time. *Not when Papa can work me like a horse.*

She trimmed and trimmed, her blisters throbbing with each swing of the hatchet. She wrestled more logs back to the house, and when her blisters broke, had her mother wrap and tie her hands with strips of cloth.

Heaving a log slightly larger than the rest, her grip slipped and she careened backwards. One shoulder collided with a broom-handle sized sapling, too small for Bram to have cut, tumbling her into the mud.

Bram stuck his axe into the tree he was chopping and ran over to her.

"Are you hurt?" he asked.

Her hands hurt, her shoulder hurt, and she was covered in mud. She stood up, furious. "What are we even doing this for?" she asked. "What good's a root cellar going to do us, anyhow, when we're just going to have to leave?"

Bram grabbed her arm. "Don't you talk that way!" Bram said. He pushed her away, and she slipped again. She plopped down, her feet splayed out in front of her.

Bram towered over her, shouting. "What would you have me do? Leave, like a dog? This is all we have, Maria. Alles! We should go back with nothing, only because Mr. Seymour says so? Nein. I will not do it!"

He turned his back on her, paced a single step, then spun to face her again. "All my work, und your mother's. Leave it? You have no idea what you are saying. We do not leave until *I* say we leave."

He seized her by both her arms yanked her back upright. He snatched up the thin end of the log like a matchstick and shoved it at her. "We need a root cellar, or we die in the winter! Every day I work, so we may survive the winter. Now you work, und not one more word from you today. Verstehst du?"

Maria nodded, her lips clamped together. She pulled the heavy log with painful hands up to the house, and the next one, and the next. When Bram went in for dinner, he glared at Maria, and she knew she was not invited.

When he passed her after eating on the way back to the bottom lands, she wanted to apologize, but the words *I'm sorry, Papa,* died on her lips.

It was true, what he said, and she knew it. The prairie wasn't like Chicago, with its grocers and apothecaries. Here, the measure of a year was whether you survived the winter. Everything turned on whether the crops came in, and if they did, on having a proper root cellar to keep them in.

So she worked. The pile at the root cellar grew, log by log, and every time she returned for the next one, she wanted to apologize.

Her blisters bled through the cloth wraps. *Dang that Mr. Seymour!* Papa was right that it wasn't for Mr. Seymour nor anyone else to tell them to leave.

Come to that, she didn't want to leave. Not really. It might be nice to live in Columbus someday, but the idea of returning to Chicago wasn't so pleasing to her anymore.

She worked all afternoon, and every time she saw her father, she wanted to say those words. She thought them, but she could not make them come out her lips.

He cut a final log, late as the sun glowed sideways through the trees, and left her there without a word. Maria looked at the remaining logs, scattered here and there across the soft, wet ground, and counted an even dozen.

The sun was down before she finished the last of them. She came inside, a sweaty, muddy mess. Everyone looked up from the table. Laisa moved to help her, but Maria only said, "I can do it," and Laisa sat back down.

Maria peeled the filthy cloth strips from her hands, wincing where they stuck to her raw blisters, and dropped them into the laundry basket. Her dress soon followed. She struggled into her nightgown, ignoring the food on the table and the ravenous hollow in her middle, and flopped into bed. She was asleep immediately.

BRAM SPENT THREE days with his adze, hewing flats onto both sides of each log. *Just like the men at the depot,* Maria thought. His hands, protected by hard calluses, did not blister. He smoothed the flats with the shiny, new drawknife and set Maria to chopping angled points onto one end of each with the hatchet.

When the logs were prepared, Maria helped hold them in the sawbuck while Bram cut them each ten feet long. The vibrations from the saw made her blisters sting. She could not bear the work with Bram still mad at her, so at last she apologized.

"Danke, Maria," Bram said. "But it may be true. Perhaps we may have to leave. I do not know."

"No, Papa! We can't leave."

"I said only I do not know. I hope not, but I must be honest also. I do not know. We must prepare for the worst *und* the best, ja? So, we make a root cellar."

Maria wasn't sure about that, but she nodded. It made some sense, what he said, but she also knew the more her father worked the homestead, the less he would ever accept leaving it. She understood that, proud as she was over the work she had put into the garden, the fields, and now the root cellar.

After apologizing, the work was almost pleasant. They cut every log with Bram's new saw, which slid through the bright, clean wood like Ma's knife through a wheel of fresh cheese. The ground beneath went white with sap-smelling sawdust.

Maria held each log in place against the inside of the root cellar, their round sides facing out. She held them while Bram pounded them like great wooden nails into the soil, until each was level with the top of the cellar's sod walls. The angled points Maria had cut made the logs snug up tight to one another. Their flat faces met so well Maria thought she could scarcely slip a blade of grass between them.

When the walls were finished, they laid the cut-off ends over the top for a roof. These Bram covered with a thick layer of straw, and finally, a bed of fresh-cut sod.

All that was left was to cut the opening to the house. This Bram had to do from the inside of the house, for the root cellar was now sealed. Bram measured carefully to the exact place on the inside wall and broke through with a few jabs of his shovel.

They made a terrible mess, carving out that opening. Laisa complained loudly about the dirt all over her floor, but there was nothing for it. Piece by piece, Bram removed chunks of sod from the walls, Maria carried them out, and Klarina swept up the leavings.

The new cellar stood empty and perfectly dark, like a cave joined onto the house. Bram cut a few final logs to length, flattened them like the others, and nailed them to crosspieces for a door. He hung it on leather loops lashed around a pole, and the root cellar was complete.

Bram stood back, admiring his work. "Tomorrow, I will go to Columbus," he said.

"What for?" Laisa asked.

"If Gott is with us, Mr. Dodge may be there. But I will go to see George Train. The reverend is right. Perhaps he can help."

CHAPTER 18

BRAM LEFT EARLY the next day. When the morning chores were done, Laisa clapped her hands once and said, "Come, girls. Today, we must make soap."

Laisa carried the ash barrel, now full to the top with soft gray ashes, outside. She stacked cut wood in layers until it was high enough, then set the barrel on top. She worked the cork stopper out of the small hole at the bottom, and set a bucket underneath the hole.

She instructed Maria in how to make the lye. She must pour water slowly down through the ashes, until it dripped out the hole and filled the bucket. Then, she must scoop the drips and pour them through the ashes, over and over, until a potato would float easily in the liquid. But she must take care not to touch the drips at all, or they would burn her even though the water was cold.

Laisa took Klarina to find herbs and flowers to mix into the soap while Maria attended to the lye.

It was interesting work at first, but soon grew dull. After a while the lye water took on a strong, sharp smell that made Maria cough.

Laisa and Klarina returned. Laisa carried sprigs of lavender, while Klarina clutched a handful of different flowers. Laisa pronounced the lye to be strong enough, so they set the bucket aside. Laisa sent Maria to the river to wash out the ash barrel, while she melted the lard.

When Maria returned, Laisa had her big cast iron kettle in the front yard, hanging from a stand. The stand was three long poles of black iron, hinged together at the top, with a chain and hook hanging down. The kettle hung from the hook, above a fire Laisa had built underneath.

Inside the kettle was all the fat Laisa had saved from last fall's plump prairie chickens, from the side of bacon they had used up in the winter, and every other wild thing they had eaten since. With that many kinds of meat Maria thought it ought to smell good, but somehow the mixture of different odors turned her stomach.

Laisa stirred with a long-handled wooden spoon as the fat melted down. She skimmed out tiny bits of old meat that floated to the top and flicked them out onto the ground. Maria took a turn, skimming as the fat went clear and began to bubble around the edges. Steam curled up out of the kettle.

She stirred and skimmed until the aroma went away, the bubbling stopped, and the steam vanished. The fire burned down low and the hot fat cooled off some. From time to time, Maria stood back while Laisa flicked a few drops of water into the pot. The water popped and snapped, and Laisa said, "Not yet."

At last, Laisa flicked the water in and nothing happened. The fat was cool enough. She sent Maria inside for the herbs and flowers, which were chopped fine and waiting inside a bowl.

"Now stand away, Schatzie, und hold Klarina's hand," she said, "while I add the lye."

Carefully, slowly, Laisa added the lye to the fat. The sharp lye smell grew strong in the yard. Maria moved around with her sister, trying to get upwind of it. Laisa called for the herbs, which she let Maria mix into the kettle.

"Now what?" Klarina asked.

"Now we stir und stir, Kleine Maus," Laisa said, "until it is soap."

Laisa stirred for a few minutes while the girls watched, then went inside to fix their midday dinner. Maria took over. She was careful not to stir too hard, lest the mixture spill over the sides.

Klarina pointed towards the wagon trail. "Look, Maria. Two men."

Maria looked, and indeed, there were two men on horseback approaching the homestead. They were still small with distance, but something made her say, "Go tell Mama." Klarina ran inside, and came out again moments later with Laisa.

The men were closer. Laisa took the long wooden spoon and said, "Go stand by the door, girls, und keep quiet." She stirred the soap as the men approached.

They stopped where the trail passed the homestead's northern marker post, talking and gesturing to one another. Then they turned their horses towards the house and rode in.

They hitched up to the paddock fence and walked over towards Laisa. They were young men. One of them was broad and thick, sandy-haired, and his trousers were held up with suspenders. The other was thin like Bram. His hair was hidden under a hat, and he wore a length of rope for a belt around his waist.

The thick one wore a pistol at his side, but it was the thin one who spoke. "You missus Browning?"

"Browning, ja," Laisa said.

"Well y'all have to git off'n this patch, y'understand? Railroad's comin' through."

Laisa cocked her head, and kept stirring. "Ich verstehe nicht. Sprechen Sie Deutsch?"

The thin one muttered, "Aw, shoot." He turned to his fellow, "You make out any of what she's saying? Silas didn't say nothin' about this."

Again, Laisa said she didn't understand—although Maria knew she very well did—and asked if the men spoke German.

The thin man pulled the hat off his head, and rolled it up in his hands. He slapped the hat against his open palm. He spoke loudly, leaning forward towards Laisa. "Y'all better clear out, less'n things git mighty warm for you. Y'understand? Go. Vamoose."

"Gehst hinein, Mädchen," Laisa said, in a clear voice. "Schliesst die Tür." *Go in. Block the door.* Maria pulled Klarina inside. She grabbed the wooden wedge they used to keep the door from swinging open, and kicked it into place.

"Come on, Klarina," she said. "We can hide in the root cellar." They ducked into the dark space. Klarina whimpered, but Maria shushed her while she shut that door, too.

From outside, she heard her mother tell the men to go. That they'd have to talk to Bram. "Lassen Sie uns in Ruhe. Mit mein Mann sprechen Sie."

The man's voice was muffled, but she could still make it out. She wondered why the big, sandy-haired man didn't say anything.

"Yeah, you send them girls in," she heard. "Most anything might happen out here." Maria did not like the edge in the man's voice, nor the tone in her mother's reply.

"Gehen Sie. Lass uns in Ruhe!"

Yes, please leave, Maria thought. She prayed the men would just go, and wished her father were there. Klarina pushed up against her and Maria held to her sister.

Then they heard a loud shot and a clang. A moment later, they heard their mother screaming.

"Mama!" Klarina cried out. Maria clapped a hand over her mouth.

"Shush now," Maria hissed in the lowest whisper she could manage. "They might come in!"

But from outside, she heard the thin man's voice yell, "Blazes, Delbert! We weren't supposed to hurt 'em none, you beef-headed fool. Not yet. Now come on!" Then she heard footsteps. And then softly, hoofbeats, and all the while, her mother's screams.

Maria let go of Klarina and raced outside.

Everything was sideways. Laisa lay on the ground. The iron kettle stand lay beside her, the kettle sprawled on its side. The mess of fat and lye had spilled out into a wide, dark patch on the ground.

Maria knelt by her mother. Tears streamed from Laisa's eyes, and she held on to her right arm with her left hand, gripping just above her elbow.

"Oh, Mama! What happened?" But Maria could see what had happened. The scalding hot soap had spilled all over her mother's arm. Her sleeve clung to her skin, a redness showing through the wet, white cloth.

"Mein Arm ist verbrüht," Laisa said, her teeth gritted together. *Burnt.* A queasy feeling settled in Maria's stomach. "Water! I'll get water!"

She fetched a bucket of clean, cold water from the well and poured it slowly over Laisa's arm. Laisa screamed at the cold, but managed to say, "No, don't stop." Maria poured three full buckets of cold water over the arm before Laisa said it was enough.

"Help me inside, Schatzie."

She helped her mother into the soddie. Laisa sat at the table while Klarina watched from the doorway of the root cellar.

"Fetch my sewing scissors. I cannot take it off. You must cut the sleeve away."

Maria nodded. She lifted up a spot of dry cloth at the wrist and cut, taking care not to touch her mother with the metal of the scissors.

When she had slit the fabric all the way to the elbow, Laisa swallowed hard and said, "All right. Now unwrap it."

Maria peeled the cloth, still sticky with lye and congealing fat, as gently as she could. Wide, pale blisters were already rising up as big as Klarina's hand. Here and there, patches of skin came free with the cloth, exposing the angry red flesh of the arm underneath.

"Oh, Mama," Maria said, over and over. "Oh, Mama."

Laisa gasped and cried out, but at last, the cloth was gone and they could look at the whole thing. The inside of her arm was the worst, oozing a clear liquid from the blisters and blood from the other places.

But beyond, on the outside of her arm, the skin was only red with heat. And in a line on the very farthest side from the spill, where the cloth had bunched up, was a line of skin in Laisa's normal pale color.

"Thank Gott for that, at least," said Laisa. "Und thank you, Schatzie. Meine gute Tochter."

Maria squeezed her eyes hard against tears. She knew she must not cry. *I have to be strong now.* Her mother was brave, but Maria knew it was a bad, bad burn.

"Mama, what do I do?"

"You must fetch me a doctor, Schatzie. Bring water for Klarina und me, then go as fast as you can."

"Yes, Mama."

It wasn't yet noon. Dinner lay half-made on the stove and counter. Columbus — and her father — were a long ways away.

She fetched the water, pulled a few carrots and a handful of green beans from the garden for her own dinner, and ran flat out towards Columbus.

One thought filled her mind. *Pebblehoof.* Her feet pounded on the trail. With Pebblehoof, she could get there and back so much faster. But she had no guarantee she could find the herd. The trail was slower, but it was a sure thing.

She ran on, arguing with herself. She reached the creek where she had fallen, pausing just long enough to quench her thirst. When she stood up, she found she had decided.

She turned, and ran off the trail into the grassland. *I have to try.*

CHAPTER 19

SHE WONDERED FOR a moment which way to go. She had not seen Pebblehoof in several days, and the herd could be any-where. But it did not matter. There was only one direction she could afford to look. She ran mostly north and a little bit east.

Two miles, she thought. If she hadn't found them after two miles, she would walk.

On she went, up and down the knolls, calling Pebblehoof by name and whistling for him. Sometimes, he would come if she whistled, but other times not.

Please, God, she prayed. *Let him come this time.*

The prairie grasses were now dry in the summer heat, and rustled against the hem of her dress. When she was thirsty she ate a bite of carrot, not caring about the dirt that clung to the root, and let the juice quench her.

The soddie was lost to sight far behind her, but there was no sign of the herd.

She stopped for a moment, to catch her wind and listen for

them. "Pebblehoof!" she called out, in the biggest voice she could manage.

Had it been two miles? She wasn't sure. She heard no hoof-beats, and could not see the herd. She ran on, counting the crests of the knolls. *Ten more, then I'll give up.*

The ten passed, and she gave herself five more. Then two, but still no sign of Pebblehoof. At last, she was sure she would not find them. *Can't waste any more time.* She could not get the sight of her mother's burnt arm, of the flesh peeking through the missing skin, out of her mind. *I must find a doctor.*

She turned as best she could reckon in the direction of Columbus and ran as fast as her legs would bear.

She lost herself in the pattern of the run, her feet beating their quick rhythm, her breath coming every few steps. She kept counting the hilltops to mark the distance. Three, then seven, then twenty.

I must be halfway to Columbus by now, she thought. But it wasn't going to be enough. She could feel herself slowing, her strength failing. Her ears were filled with the sounds of her own motion and the rushing of her blood in her ears.

But under those noises, beyond them, she thought she heard an echo of her footsteps. She wondered what could be making an echo. There were no buildings or cliffs nearby. Just open, rolling prairie, all the way to the sky.

It's not an echo, she realized. The rhythm was different. It was a rhythm she knew as well as her own heartbeat, but it was not her own rhythm.

It was Pebblehoof's.

She slowed to a stop and turned around. Behind her, she saw the most beautiful sight in the world. The white blaze running down the middle of Pebblehoof's long face.

He stopped beside her.

"Oh, Pebblehoof, you heard me!" She reached up and hugged his great wide neck, and he knelt for her. She swung herself up into her seat, and urged him into motion. "Come on, boy. We must hurry."

PEBBLEHOOF'S LONG STRIDES drank up the distance like water. Maria's hair whipped behind her in the wind. Soon they were dropping down to the Loup River, with Columbus close on the other side.

The river was even lower than when she and Bram had crossed it, and Pebblehoof forded it without Maria's feet even getting wet. She rode in to town, wondering where she might find a doctor.

As she passed the railroad office, she saw two men standing close to one another on the side of the building. Her heart fluttered, thinking they were the same men from earlier, but a moment later she could tell that they were not. One had his back to her, but the other one was Mr. Harper. His back was up against the sawn-board siding.

She hopped down from Pebblehoof, keeping one hand in his mane to lead him. "Mr. Harper," she called out.

But as she came close, the other man turned. It was Mr. Seymour. His hand was knotted up in the front of Mr. Harper's shirt and his lip was curled.

Mr. Harper would help her, she knew. But Mr. Seymour was a railroad man, and it was railroad men who had hurt her mother. She did not know quite what to do.

"Leave off, girlie," Mr. Seymour growled.

But she needed that doctor. "Please, sirs," she blurted out, "Mr. Harper, I need to find a doctor. And fast!"

"Well get on and find him, then," Mr. Seymour said. "And keep your nose out of other folks' business."

"But—" she started to speak again, but stopped at a tiny shake of Mr. Harper's head.

Mr. Harper said, "You ask on down to Mr. LeClerc's store. You ain't to worry 'bout me none. Mr. Seymour and I are just talking a little business. It's all right. Go on, now."

She stammered out a quick thank you and led Pebblehoof down the street.

The door to LeClerc's Dry Goods and Trading Post was closed. Maria dared not let go of Pebblehoof to go in. She thought he would probably stay with her, but she couldn't take any chances. Not now.

She took a deep breath. "Mr. LeClerc," she shouted, as loud as she could. "Come quick, please!" She shouted it a second time, and then a third, before Mr. LeClerc came out.

"What eez it?" he asked.

"Sir, it's Maria Browning. You remember? The baskets? I need a doctor, sir."

"Un docteur? Is it your father?" he asked. "But, he was here one hour ago only."

"No, sir. It's my mama. She's been burnt."

"Mon dieu! Docteur Hastings, he eez at ze blacksmith's house. Madame Nelson, she will 'ave her baby tonight, I hear."

Mr. LeClerc told her how to find the blacksmith's house. "Allez! Hurry now," he told her. "Bonne chance!"

The blacksmith's house was easy to find, just out behind the smithy. She was glad Mr. Nelson was not whanging away at the forge, for fear the noise would spook Pebblehoof.

She listened for a crying baby, hoping Doctor Hastings was through. Instead, she heard a woman cry out in a long, tortured cry, then fall silent. It was a different kind of cry than her mother had made.

"Doctor!" Maria yelled. "Mr. Nelson, I need the doctor."

The blacksmith came out, a wild look in his eyes. His hair was tousled every which way, and he looked exceedingly fraught. "He's busy, girl. Now go on home."

Then an old man came out, skinny but spry. He wore spectacles and his hair floated in pure white wisps over his head. He laid a bony hand on Mr. Nelson's shoulder. "It's all right, Charles," he said. "Why don't you go on inside and hold your wife's hand. I'll just be a minute."

"Thank you," Maria said. Mr. Nelson nodded and went back inside.

"I do only have a minute," said the doctor, "before she'll need me again. Now what can I do for you?"

"It's my mama, sir," Maria said. "She's been burnt real bad."

"Well don't you fret. I've seen many a burn in my day, and I know a few things. Now first — "

"Doc," came Mr. Nelson's frantic voice from inside.

"Wait right here," he said. "I'll be back in two shakes."

Maria nodded, and the doctor vanished back into the house.

Maria hugged Pebblehoof again. "Do you think he can help?" Pebblehoof snuffled, and began to nose at the pocket of her dress, which still held a half a carrot and the beans.

"You're right. Where are my manners?" She gave Pebblehoof the carrot. "You deserve a whole bushel of carrots, for coming to me like that. Right when I needed you." She stroked the glossy hair under Pebblehoof's mane.

The doctor came back out. "Now, Miss. What's your name?" She told him. "Start at the beginning, but talk quick."

As fast as she could, she described what had happened.

"Did you get a good look at the burn?" he asked.

"Yes, Doctor."

"Call me Doc. Saves time."

She described what she had seen, then he interrupted again. "Two shakes. I'll be back to tell you what to do." And he was gone once more.

The waiting was awful. Inside, the woman screamed again and begged God to make it stop.

Then Doc Hastings was back. He wasted no time, talking the second his foot was out the door. "Listen up now. First thing, you have to wash all the lye off. And I mean every bit."

"I did already."

"Good, but wash it again. It'll eat away at her if you don't get it all. She won't like it, but you have to do it. Make sure no traces remain."

"I will."

"Make up a sagewort poultice. Just the leaves and water. Can you do that?" Maria nodded. "Good girl. Apply it all over the whole arm, and wrap it in cloth if you have to. Give her cone-flower root, too, if you have any. You got all that?"

"Yes, sir."

"Tell it back to me."

Maria repeated the instructions, just as he had told her, and added, "I'll make her some willow tea, too."

"Good. But do the poultice first. I'll come when I can to tend her myself. Now how do I—"

He ran inside again, and was gone longer this time. Mrs. Nelson screamed two times before he returned.

"Now how do I find you?" he asked.

"Just go west on the wagon trail," Maria said. "We're the first homestead, just where the trail meets the Platte river. On the left."

"I'll come when I can. You hurry back, now."

He went back to Mrs. Nelson without even saying goodbye. Maria mounted up and rode hard down the middle of Main Street, all the way out of town.

CHAPTER 20

A s PEBBLEHOOF FORDED back over the Loup River, she remembered something Mr. LeClerc had said. Bram had been at the store just an hour or so before her. He would have been walking back on the trail, while she had come from the west through the wild prairie, so she had missed him. She would surely meet him on the ride back.

He'll be mad about Pebblehoof.

She thought about trying to ride around him, through the grass. But the trail was the shortest way home, and she couldn't bear to make her mother suffer one more minute longer than she had to. Nor poor Klarina, who was probably scared and crying too.

She would just have to take her punishment, whatever it was, and that was that. So long as she got back soon, she could bear the rest.

Sure enough, after a while she spotted her father up ahead. "Papa," she called out. She saw him stop, raise his hand to shield his eyes from the sun, and look around. By the time he heard her coming from behind him and turned, she could see the look of surprise on his face.

She brought Pebblehoof up to a stop beside him.

"Maria!" he snapped. "You were not to ride this horse any-more."

"I know, Papa. But it's Mama. She's hurt!"

"What?" She saw the fury drain out of his eyes, replaced by sudden worry. "Tell me, Schatzie."

"She got burned making soap. It was Mr. Seymour's men what did it. Mama sent me to fetch the doctor, but he can't come right now. He told me what to do, though. I have to go."

"Ja, ja. You ride. Go fast! I will run."

Bram slapped Pebblehoof's flank, hard. Pebblehoof shot for-ward, and Maria almost tumbled off his back. She clamped on with her legs until she could regain her seat.

She leaned forward. "Faster, boy. I know you're tired, but please." Pebblehoof flew onward, and Maria tried to settle her-self into his motion, to move like she was a part of him, until she felt it was her flying over the land.

Everything faded away. The sky, the land, the staccato hoof-beats. Even time seemed to pause, leaving her with nothing but the motion of the ride.

A jostle brought her back to herself, just in time to see the dark line of the creek bed up ahead. *I can't fall now.* She leaned back a notch. "Slow down, boy. We're almost there."

Pebblehoof slowed out of his full gallop. She brought him down to a trot, and he splashed through the stream. Moments later, she was riding onto the homestead, past the four acres, and into the soddie's front yard.

"Mama!" she called out.

She dismounted. "Thank you, Pebblehoof." She kissed his broad nose. "I have to go," she said, and she ran inside.

SHE FOUND HER mother in bed. Laisa's face was pale. She had arranged a chair near the bed, and rested her hand upon the chair so her burned arm didn't have to touch anything. Maria found her sister hiding in the root cellar, crying but silent.

"Maria?" Laisa's voice sounded weak. "Where is the doctor?"

"I'm sorry. He's delivering a baby. But he told me what to do, and he'll come when he can." She explained Doc Hastings' instructions, and Laisa nodded.

"It hurts, Schatzie. My lord, it hurts."

"I know, Mama. I'll get you some willow tea, just as soon as I can. But I have to tend to you first."

Maria set a tin washtub under Laisa's arm. She fetched bucket after bucket of water from the well, pouring them to wash the lye off. Laisa gritted her teeth and moaned, her face growing even paler.

When the washtub was full, Maria declared the burn cleaned. She flitted about the kitchen, snatching up the jar of sagewort, a kettle, and the mortar and pestle.

She set the kettle on to boil and threw a handful of kindling sticks into the oven. She dumped as much sagewort into the mortar as would fit, and began grinding it down. When the water was hot, she added it, a splash at a time, and continued grinding until she had a dark green paste.

She fetched a butter knife and carried the mortar over to the bedside. "I have to spread this on your arm, now."

Laisa nodded, her lips squeezed tight together. But at the first touch of the thick poultice on Laisa's raw flesh, she cried out. Maria jerked the butter knife away.

"I'm sorry, Mama," Maria said. A frantic feeling came up in her. *This is all wrong*, she thought. *I shouldn't have to do this.* But she did. There wasn't anyone else, at least, not till Papa got home. She brought the knife back towards her mother's arm.

"Wait," Laisa whispered. "Spread it on a cloth, und wrap it around."

Maria rifled through her mother's rag bin, looking for a piece of cloth big enough to do the job. She found one, a threadbare stretch of cotton print with a pattern of green leaves that she recognized from a dress she once wore and Klarina wore out.

She spread the poultice on the cloth. Laisa still cried out when Maria wrapped it around her arm, but at least it was over quickly. She lightly tied a few long rag strips around to hold the poultice in place, then helped her mother move her arm ever so carefully to lie beside her on the bed.

"Danke, Schatzie," Laisa said. "I am sorry for crying out."

"Shh, Mama. Just you rest, and I'll take care of you."

She prepared a dose of coneflower root, which Laisa took without complaint, and used the rest of the hot water to brew a large pot of willow tea.

Her mother grimaced at the bitter taste, but drank down every bit. In a while the color began to return to her cheeks. She sat up and had Maria tell her again exactly what Doc Hastings had said, and all about her trip to and from Columbus.

Bram arrived, panting and out of breath, just as Maria finished. She had to tell the whole thing over once more while her father caught his wind, only this time from when the two thugs had arrived at the house.

"The Devil take that Mr. Seymour und his men!" Bram said. "I'll have his hide for this."

"Bram," Laisa said, her voice quiet. "You will do no such thing. Do not make things worse."

"I should have been here," Bram said. "This would not have happened."

"You don't know that. It could have been something worse."

"Worse? You might lose your arm, Liebe! How could it be worse?" Bram asked. "How?"

Maria grew suddenly cold. *Lose her arm? Please, God, not that.*

"One of them had a gun," Laisa said. "He shot, I think only to frighten me, but the bullet hit the kettle stand und it fell. It could have been much worse."

"But all of this, für nichts und wieder nichts! Mr. Train, he will not help. He has no warm feeling for Mr. Seymour, but he needs the railroad. Everyone does. He will not risk crossing Mr. Seymour. I tell you, I will not waste one more day like this. Not one."

It was a long and terrible night. The pain grew worse with each passing hour, until it surpassed the comfort of willow tea. Laisa sank out of awareness and back in, crying out with every movement, but could not truly sleep for the pain.

Bram and Maria tended her as best they could, though there was little they could do.

When dawn came, spreading its grey light into the western sky, Maria was as weary as ever she could remember. But she had not even finished fixing breakfast when they heard the sound of a horse clopping into the yard.

Maria peeked through the window and saw the wispy white hair of the man dismounting.

"It's the doctor! Papa, he's here."

Bram stirred from his own fitful sleep in the chair by the bed-side, while Maria threw open the door. She ushered Doc Hastings inside, and made quick introductions to her parents. Doc waved a smiling hello to Klarina, who retreated back to the safety of the root cellar.

Despite the early hour, Doc Hastings seemed as fresh as ever. Maria wondered when he must have left Columbus to arrive so early. He sat himself down on the chair next to Laisa, his black leather bag at his feet, and talked while he looked over Maria's handiwork with the poultice.

"I'm sorry to keep her waiting so long," Doc said. "But I just couldn't leave the Nelsons. Poor Mrs. Nelson. The baby was breech. She tried so hard, she did. But she gave out, and curse it, I couldn't get the baby out in time. Let us keep Mr. Nelson in our prayers."

"Och. The poor man," Bram said. Maria did not know what to say.

"Don't you fret, though. I don't aim to lose anybody else today." He gently untied the rags around the poultice, and carefully peeled away one corner of it. He took a pinch of the poultice between his fingers and gave it a sniff.

"This is nicely done, Miss Browning. A little more water in the poultice next time, though. Goes on easier if it's softer, and it works a little better too."

Bram and Maria stood close, watching. Bram held one arm around Maria, hugging her to him.

Doc Hastings opened his bag and rummaged through it, producing a small brown bottle. "I want you to take a draught of laudanum, Mrs. Browning. It's a darned sight less palatable than willow tea, but it'll ease the pain and help you sleep."

Laisa choked and coughed at the medicine, but swallowed it down.

"We'll just give her a while before what comes next," Doc said.

It did not take long. In minutes, Laisa drifted into sleep.

"Thank Gott for that," Bram murmured.

"Indeed so," said Doc. "She would not thank us to do this bit while she's awake. Miss Browning, fetch me clean water and a basin."

Maria did, and watched while he removed the poultice wrap and washed her mother's arm clean. More and larger pieces of skin sloughed free into the wash water, and some he trimmed with small scissors.

Doc clicked his tongue and shook his head, looking this way and that over every part of the arm.

"Well, now, here's a piece of good news," he said when he came to the line of unburned skin on the outside edge of Laisa's arm. "See here, this is live skin, all the way from her elbow up to her hand. That is indeed a blessing."

"Why?" Bram asked.

"The rest of it'll die off, but it'll grow back from what remains. With this line to start from, she'll heal much faster. It's early days, but if you can keep it from going sour she ought to keep her arm."

"What must we do?" Bram asked. "Anything."

"Well first, Miss Browning, let's make up a fresh poultice." Doc mixed up another batch with the remaining sagewort to show Maria the proper consistency, then talked her through the best way to apply it.

"Now then," Doc said, "you take that darling little girl in the root cellar and teach her how to find sagewort. You're going to need a lot of it. Miss Browning, every night, you clean her arm just like I did and apply fresh poultice on a clean cloth. In the morning, and at midday and evening, douse the whole thing with strong spirits. It'll smart like the dickens, but spirits have a cooling effect on the burn. Give her laudanum as she needs it, but not too much. Just a spoonful, like I did.

"Do that for a week, then let it stay out in the air a little while each day till it scabs over. Sunshine's good, too. Keep it uncovered and dry after that. I'll come back in a fortnight to see how she's getting on."

He gave them the bottle of laudanum, which he said ought to last the week, and stayed to breakfast. Bram paid him five whole dollars for the medicine. Maria knew what five dollars meant. *A lot more baskets.*

Bram and Maria waved as Doc Hastings rode away. "Thank Gott for that," Bram said. "She will keep her arm."

God willing, Maria thought. *And if I take care of her proper.*

CHAPTER 21

WHILE LAISA RECOVERED, Bram redoubled his efforts to prepare the homestead for the coming winter. He laid in a good supply of wood and hay. He built shelves in the root cellar so they could fill it floor to ceiling with baskets of carrots, turnips, potatoes, and cabbages from the garden.

He tended to the four acres, which were near ready to harvest. The sixteen acres that were planted late, he said, ought to ripen if the weather held out another week or two. He even planted his orchard with English walnuts Mr. LeClerc ordered for him special all the way from New York City.

Maria took care of her mother. The laudanum kept Laisa in bed, but was a blessing as Maria could change the poultice while she slept. She kept the house, cooked the meals, and washed the laundry. On Saturday, she hauled and boiled water for their baths.

For her part, Klarina proved to have an eagle-eye for sagewort. Every day, she brought home bunches of fresh plants for Maria to grind into poultice.

All the while, Maria wondered what her punishment would be for having carried on with Pebblehoof despite her father's orders. Bram had said nothing of it, but she knew he would not forget.

After a week, the laudanum ran out and Laisa's arm had formed a scab. Laisa did not complain, but asked often for willow bark tea. Maria could see the pain on her mother's face, and wished she could do something to take it away.

The first evening Laisa was well enough to take supper at the table, she said, "Bless you, Maria. Und thank you. I do not know what I would have done without you." She squeezed Maria's arm with her good hand.

"Ja," Bram said. "But there is still the matter of the horse. This Pebblehoof. You disobeyed me, Schatzie."

Maria looked down at her plate. "I know, Papa. I'm sorry."

"I am not," Laisa said, her voice stronger than it had been in weeks. "Two times, Bram, Maria and her horse have saved us. We will have wheat and corn, because of that horse. I will have my arm because of him. Ja she should be obedient, but she did what she must und I am not sorry."

"This is true," Bram said, and he was silent a long while. "So. Maria, your punishment for disobeying is that you will not leave our land until your mother is fully recovered. Und until then, you will keep the house. I do not want your mother using her arm until it is well once more."

It was hardly any punishment at all. *I'm doing all of that anyhow.* Maria almost smiled, but kept her face still. "Yes, Papa," she said.

Maria ate in silence. Her parents talked of what they might buy for winter with the money from their crops, but Maria wasn't listening. She could only think of one thing. Pebblehoof. Would she be allowed to ride him anymore?

The meal ended and Maria could stand it no longer. One way or the other, she had to know.

"Papa?"

"Ja, Schatzie?"

"May I— I mean, when Mama's well again—"

"What is it?"

"What about Pebblehoof?"

Bram looked to Laisa, and Maria saw something pass between them. Then Bram said, "Ja. When your mother is well, if the herd has not moved on, you may ride him."

Maria threw her arms around her father's waist. "Oh, thank you, Papa!"

That evening, it was a joy to wash the supper dishes.

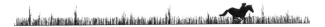

THE DAYS SETTLED into a routine of chores. Breakfast, milking and tending the animals, dinner, washing and mending and other housekeeping, supper, and dishes. In the evenings, Maria wove baskets.

Laisa, cooped up in the soddie with nothing to do, tried to weave as well. But the motions pained her and cracked the scab over her arm, so she could not. She took to walking with Klarina in the prairie, showing Klarina other useful plants and herbs. Klarina would pick, while Laisa carried the gathering basket. "That I can do with one hand," she said.

Day by day, the summer drifted towards fall. Bram harvested the wheat on the four acres and threshed it, filling so many burlap sacks with the fat red kernels that they had to stack them in Jess's old stall.

New skin slowly grew in from the edges of Laisa's burn. Maria made baskets enough for the root cellar, and when that was full, began stacking them in a corner by the wood box. She made bushel baskets, as those would fetch the best price from Mr. LeClerc, and she reckoned he'd need many of them to sell as folks put up their produce for winter.

Only once, while Maria was tending the animals in the morning, did she see the herd. To the east, the land sloped down as it followed the Platte River. Far away, under the rising sun, she caught a glimpse of the herd's dark cloud-shape moving down to the river to drink. She watched them, longing to drop the pitchfork from her hand and run after them. To leap up on Pebblehoof's broad back, to ride far and fast with her hair blowing behind her.

But she minded her father and stayed where she was.

One day early into September, as the sun struggled to melt the early autumn chill from the air, she saw Bram running pell-mell for the house. He burst through the door just long enough to snatch his rifle off of its pegs.

"Papa, what is it?"

Bram's teeth were clenched and his lips drawn back. "Are your mother and sister still out?"

Maria nodded. They had gone towards Mr. Harper's, in search of a patch of sorrel.

"Gut. It is that Mr. Seymour." He dashed back out again.

"Oh, no," Maria whispered. Quickly, she pawed through the rag bin, snatching up three shreds of cloth she deemed long enough and clean enough for bandages. *Just in case*, she thought.

She watched from the doorway. Outside, Bram stood near the stable with his legs apart, his rifle lowered but at the ready. Mr. Seymour approached, the outline of his wide-brimmed hat dark against the sky behind him.

Before he even dismounted, Bram called out, "Get off my land."

"Now, don't be so hasty, Mr. Browning," said Mr. Seymour. He slid down out of his saddle, but made no move to hitch his horse to the paddock fence.

"What do you want, then?" Bram asked.

"I wanted to say I heard what happened to Mrs. Browning. Terrible accident, that must have been. I came out to see if I might buy you out of your claim. At a more reasonable price."

"I said get off my land."

"I know we had some harsh words before, but let's put all that in the past, shall we? What do you say to two hundred and fifty dollars."

Bram yanked back the hammer on the rifle. "Two hundred und fifty dollars? For my home? For my land? For a year of my sweat und labor? Your men almost kill meine Frau und you would insult me with this offer?"

"Tarnation, Browning! It's the best you'll get. Anything can happen out here. Horse thieves. Prairie fires. A man never knows. You best take it, before your family has any more accidents."

Bram raised his rifle. "Get off my land now, you fieser Dreksack!" Bram said. Maria wasn't sure what those words meant, but she reckoned she could guess.

"I will warn you one time only," he added. "I am an excellent marksman."

"Put down the rifle, Mr. Browning." Mr. Seymour pulled a roll of paper money from his pocket and held it up for Bram to see. "Two hundred and fifty dollars. Cash in hand. Last chance."

The rifle sounded with a crack, and a cloud of smoke shot up from the chamber. Mr. Seymour's hat went flying backwards, tumbling into the dirt. Mr. Seymour ducked down, too late to make any difference to anything, and his horse spooked.

"Gol durn you, you crazy Hessian!" Mr. Seymour ran after

his horse, which was trotting around the paddock fence. "You'll regret that!"

"I aim lower next time, ja?" Bram yelled back. He flipped the rifle around, gripping it like a club, and gave chase. "Now get off my land or I will beat you, so help me Gott!"

Mr. Seymour whistled for his horse while he ran. He threw himself into the saddle, yelled "H'ya!" and rode away.

Bram stood beside the paddock fence, watching, until Mr. Seymour was nothing but a dark speck on the distance of the wagon trail. He picked up Mr. Seymour's hat and came inside.

Bram re-loaded the rifle. He tried to sit for a cup of willow tea, but couldn't. He left the cup on the table, took up the rifle, and paced around the yard, watching, until Laisa and Klarina returned.

Maria laid out settings on the supper table. Laisa set Klarina to tying bundles of sorrel up to dry, and asked, "Whose hat is that?"

"Mr. Seymour's."

Laisa picked up the hat, and looked at the two holes Bram's bullet had left.

"And where is Mr. Seymour?" The worry was plain on her face.

Bram shrugged. "Columbus, by now." He told her what had happened.

Laisa shook her head. "Let us be thankful no one was hurt," she said. "But Bram, you should not have done this."

"After what his men did to you? I should have—"

Laisa glared at him, her lips tight and straight across her face.

"Ja, ja," Bram said. "You are right. But there is nothing for it now. What will come, will come."

AND COME IT did. Soon, Bram declared the sixteen acres to be ripe. He came in for supper, saying, "Early to bed, Maria. Tomorrow we will begin the harvest."

Maria awoke the following morning to a banging noise. *Time to rise already?* Her body was heavy with sleep. "Papa?" she murmured. Dawn was only just blushing through the soddie's window.

But as she heard Bram jumping out of bed, she smelled it. *Smoke.*

Bram threw open the door. "Oh, Mein Gott!" he shouted. "Fire, Laisa! Mädchen! Come quickly!"

Maria rushed outside, coughing on thick smoke. The sixteen acres of corn and wheat were in flames. She felt the heat on her face even from the doorway.

Bram ran out while Laisa directed the girls to pull every quilt and blanket from the beds. "Bring them all to the well," she ordered.

They soaked the blankets with buckets of water. Laisa cried out as the scabs on her arm cracked and tore from the effort of lifting the heavy buckets.

Bram was back in moments. "We cannot save it, but we may yet save the garden. Kleine Maus, you und your mother protect the house. Maria, we must beat at the flames." He grabbed a dripping wet blanket and braced himself while Laisa threw a bucket of water on him. Maria did the same, gasping at the shock of icy water drenching her in her nightshirt.

Pebblehoof! Maria thought. What if the fire escaped onto the prairie? She wanted to run up to the wagon trail, to beat the flames back on that side. But they had to save the garden. If they lost that, they would starve over the winter.

Mercifully, the breeze that morning blew towards the river, driving the flames away from the trail. Bram and Maria beat at the fire's margins, rushing back and forth around the garden as sparks jumped and started new fires ever closer.

Maria's lungs burned with the smoke. Her eyes stung and watered. She could not catch her breath for coughing, and her legs soon felt like jelly with the effort of running. They followed the fire's edge as it moved before the breeze, keeping the worst of it away from the homestead.

At last, the fire burned itself out in the moist bottom lands near the river, where the grasses were still green. The morning sun, just up in the east, shone blood-red through the lingering smoke. Bram dropped to his knees, thanking God that the fire had not jumped into the trees on the river banks.

Only when Bram was certain the fire was well and truly out did they return to the soddie. The breeze blew the smoke away, but not the smell. Maria gasped for breath as they emerged into clear air, her throat raw and ragged.

They dropped their soggy, blackened blankets in a heap. Laisa handed something to Bram. Maria blinked her watery eyes clear, and saw it was a piece of paper.

"It was nailed to the door," Laisa said.

So that was the banging noise, Maria thought. She didn't need to ask who had left it. "What's it say, Papa?" she asked.

Bram crumpled the paper and shoved it in his pocket. "It does not matter," he said. "They cannot chase us away so easily, ja?"

CHAPTER 22

SEPTEMBER GAVE A flare of Indian summer. The air grew warm for a handful of lovely days, marred only by the lingering smell of smoke and the ugly, burned streak of land running down to the river.

Doc Hastings visited as the warmth ceded to the chill of fall, and declared that Laisa was almost fully healed. The areas where the burn had been mildest were almost their normal color again. The rest was a mottle of reds and purples, with just a few fingernail-sized patches of whitish scab remaining.

"You may begin to use it again, Mrs. Browning," he told her. "In fact, you should. Don't fear to work it as much as you're able. You must build the strength back in it."

He also gave her instructions to stretch her arm out fully, several times every day, though it would be painful. "You must stretch it now, while it heals. Otherwise, the scar will pull it up tight like a chicken wing, and you'll lose the full use of it."

Laisa set to winter preparations with a vengeance. With Maria and Klarina both helping, she brought in bushel after bushel of cabbage, hard squash, and root vegetables. The root cellar was filled for winter. The last two baskets of beets and carrots would not fit inside.

"I suppose you und your father should have made a bigger cellar," said Laisa.

"Yes, Mama," said Maria. But she remembered the agony of hauling those logs up from the riverbed and was glad they hadn't.

"Well. We will have to put up these extras. They will not keep here in the warm part of the house."

Bram promised to go to Columbus as soon as he could to fetch pickling supplies.

On the next morning, frost descended on the land. Maria woke to delicate frost ferns on the window, reaching in from the edges towards the center of the glass. Frost covered the ground with a layer of white that sparkled in the clear morning light. Glints of color jumped to her eyes from every direction as she fetched water for breakfast.

There would be no more warm days until spring, but Maria didn't mind. Her mother was well—for which she was exceedingly glad—but more than that, her punishment was at an end.

She ate and completed her morning chores as fast as she was able. Before Bram even came in for dinner, she asked, "Mama, may I go out?"

Laisa hugged Maria with two arms, for the first time in what felt like forever. "Ja, Schatzie. Go und find your Pebblehoof. But be home—"

Maria didn't wait. She bolted for the door. "—for supper! I will!"

She did not find the herd that day, but did on the next. They were west, past Mr. Harper's place. She whistled and Pebblehoof came running like no time at all had passed.

She threw her arm around his neck and buried her face in his warm mane, drawing in the scent of him. "Oh, it's so good to see you, Pebblehoof," she said. She petted his nose. "Did you miss me?"

Pebblehoof nickered and looked at her with his dark, dark eyes. *Let's run,* he seemed to be saying, or maybe she only imagined it, but before she knew it she was in her familiar seat high in the air and they were off. She jolted at the first few trotting steps, before recollecting her movements, then leaned in to Pebblehoof's silk-smooth rhythm as he built into a gallop.

She rode up the wagon trail, past Mr. Harper's place, then on past her own homestead. Bram was out with Poppy, plowing the blackened fields under. She whooped and waved as they passed by. Bram turned to look, but did not take his hands off the plow to wave.

The cold air chapped her lips and her cheeks, and brought tears into her eyes, but she did not ask Pebblehoof to slow down. On they went until Maria was exhausted from riding and laughing, giddy with the joy of it.

That evening, Laisa used the last of the willow switches on a basket, but ran out before it was complete.

"I'll get more tomorrow," Maria offered, though she knew it would be work. They had harvested so much willow from the riverbanks closest to the house that all the fresh, thin switches were gone for quite a distance.

Then she thought, *Pebblehoof can help me, now I'm allowed.* She set out the next afternoon with a few lengths of twine and a cutting knife, wrapped carefully in a piece of rag and tucked into her dress pocket.

She gave Pebblehoof his head, not caring where he went. He

took her north, across the heart of the prairie, towards the Loup River. She called out to him, over the wind and the pounding of his hooves, "It's a wonder, but I think I shall never tire of this."

They turned at the Loup, back south, and rode slower. Maria nudged left and right, until they reached a stand of willow at the western edge of the homestead. She led Pebblehoof down to the river to drink, and talked to keep him nearby while she cut switches.

By and by, she had a great pile of good, thin willow, new growth from that very spring. The pile, she reckoned, would fill the soaking barrel. Maybe more. She lashed it with twine into a fat, round bundle.

She whistled for Pebblehoof to come over, so she could lift it up onto his back. She led him gently to where she needed him, then found she could not lift the bundle. She tried wrapping both arms around it, and while she could rock it to and fro, she couldn't heave it from the ground.

She tried working both arms under it from the bottom, and a great many other methods, but it was no use. It was simply more than she could lift.

She sat down on the cold bundle, breathing hard.

"It's too bad you don't have hands," she said. Pebblehoof looked down at her, and nibbled a bit from the end of one of the switches.

She pondered what to do. If she could get the bundle onto his back, the rest would be easy.

She thought a while, and said, "All right, boy. I need you to kneel down for me now." She pressed gently down on his withers, like she used to before she could mount as easily as she could now. Pebblehoof obligingly lowered himself down.

"Good. Now just stay there, won't you?"

She worked her fingers into one end of the bundle and heaved with all her might. Her arms strained, her back and her legs strained, but she managed to tip the bundle upright.

"Steady now," she said, as she carefully eased the bundle over to lean on Pebblehoof's side. He squirmed and tried to stand, but she put one hand on his withers again. "Stay down. That's good."

When Pebblehoof seemed ready, she squatted down next to the bundle and took hold of it. "Now don't you move," she said, and she lifted.

It was a close thing. The bundle was heavy and awkward, and threatened to roll and tip every which way. But she did not let go and at last had it up onto his back without it tumbling over the other side.

"Come on up," she said. She clicked her tongue and Pebblehoof stood up.

He rose quickly, taking a step forward and pitching the bundle towards the other side. Maria clung to it, adding her weight to keep it from falling. "Steady," she said, while she wrestled the bundle back into place.

With the willow balanced on Pebblehoof's back, and Maria keeping a firm hold on it, they walked the half mile back to the soddie.

On the way into the yard, they passed Bram pitching spent hay and cow dung onto the manure pile. "Mein Gott, Maria," he called out. "What is that?"

Maria smiled at him. "It's ten dollars' worth of bushel baskets," she said, "and willow bark to last all winter."

When they reached the house, Maria let the bundle drop to the ground. The twine split, but it was no matter.

"Good boy, Pebblehoof," she said, and she scratched under his mane. "I would have taken three days to carry that much back here myself."

She fetched a handful of carrots from the root cellar, and fed them to him as she led him back out to the wagon trail.

"Bye now," she said. "I have to set all that into the soaking barrel. And I ought to help fix supper. But I'll see you."

Pebblehoof snuffled, his hot breath making a cloud in the cool afternoon air.

"Stay close, will you?" Maria asked. She knew the words wouldn't mean anything to him, but hoped what Mr. Harper had said so long ago was true. She hoped Pebblehoof understood more than he let on.

He crunched the last bite of carrot and trotted off.

A COLD WIND blew up, bringing an early dusting of snow. Not much, just enough to leave everything white. But it reminded Maria of the long, dark winter days she had spent in the soddie before spring came.

Maria and Laisa stayed indoors weaving baskets. Klarina helped by stripping the bark from the switches and splitting them down the middle. Laisa's fingers were still nimble and quick—the soap had not burned them—but her arm tired quickly so she did not work long at a stretch.

It was nice, working with her mother, and Maria was proud of her mother's skill. In Chicago, she'd never known her mother could make baskets, and would certainly never have had the chance to learn it herself.

She was proud of her own skill too—her baskets were now every bit as good as Laisa's—but she would never say that out loud. Laisa taught her how to weave patterns of stripes and diamonds into the sides. A zigzag pattern made her think of lightning.

On the next clear, sunny day, Bram went to Columbus. He

hitched Poppy to the wagon and left to fetch jars, salt, sugar, and a jug of vinegar for pickling the extra beets and cabbages.

The early snow did not last, and was gone before he returned that afternoon. The wagon was laden with supplies, but Bram did not look happy.

Maria went out to help carry things inside. "What's the matter, Papa?"

"Don't ask questions," he said. "I will tell you all inside."

When the wagon was empty and Poppy was back in her stall, Bram came in.

"What is it, Bram?" Laisa asked.

"Mr. Seymour has withdrawn his offer," Bram said.

Laisa snorted. "So? Did you expect anything different? It was a terrible offer anyway."

"But that is not the worst of it. One of his men was at LeClerc's, und went to fetch him. He says now he will blacklist us if we do not leave."

There was a silence around the table, then Laisa said, "Heaven help us."

"What?" Klarina asked. Maria tried to shush her, but it was no good. "What is blacklist, Papa?"

"It means if we do not do what he says, he will stop us from doing business with anyone, from here all the way to Omaha."

"What?" Maria could not help herself. "But he can't do that!"

"I fear he can, Schatzie. It is not a right thing, but he can do it. Everyone needs the railroad, und Mr. Seymour *is* the railroad. It is why Mr. Train would not help us, I think. Everyone must buy und sell what they make, und everything must go by rail. If he says no one must buy from us, no one must sell to us, that is how it will be. No one will risk also to be blacklisted for helping us."

Maria thought about it. "I see. If we leave, we have to start over somewhere else. And if we stay, we won't ever be able to make enough money for you to get your print shop."

"Nein. If we leave, we *cannot* start over somewhere else. There is no money, und we cannot sell our claim. Who would buy a homestead the railroad will only destroy?" Bram laughed, short and sharp. "What even was the use of planting all those trees?"

No one answered him. "Would we have to go back to Chicago?" Maria asked.

Bram and Laisa exchanged a look. "Ja. Back to Chicago. I am sorry, meine Lieben. I should have worked something out with him sooner."

A hole opened in Maria's heart. *Chicago.* Papa would go back to the print shop, if he could still get a job there. Mama would go back to the factories. *And I'd have to go too.* It was almost too much to bear. Once, she would have liked to go back to Chicago. But now, it was different. The rolling grass, the wide skies, even the dirt floor of the soddie — these were a part of her now. She understood how her father felt. She would not let them go.

And Pebblehoof, she thought. *I'll never leave him behind.*

"No, Papa. Let him do it, then!" Maria said. "We should stay, even if he does blacklist us. We can live here just fine, can't we?"

"Perhaps, Schatzie. I do not know." He turned to Laisa. "What do you say?"

"I say you were right not to give in. It is our land, und we have two fine strong girls to work it. I will not see them in the mills, to go deaf at the looms." She glanced down at her scarred arm. "Or worse."

Bram took a deep breath. He smiled at them, and Maria almost thought she saw tears building at the corners of his eyes. "Ja, we will stay! Und when the walnuts grow, we can eat them."

He gave Maria a squeeze around her shoulders. "Still, there

is some good news. I told Mr. LeClerc about your bushel baskets, und he said he will buy as many as you can supply. Mr. Seymour will not blacklist us yet. Not for a little while, anyway. So you weave fast, ja? We will need the money."

CHAPTER 23

THE FIELDS WERE put to bed for the winter. Bram busied himself with increasing their store of firewood, until the split logs piled high right outside the front door. He even cut a few poles and stretched canvas over them to make a woodshed. "I must cut sod for walls next year," he said, "But this will keep the wood dry enough."

He sharpened and oiled all his tools, fixed and mended every little thing that had become worn through summer's use. Laisa put up jars and jars of pickled beets. She sliced the extra heads of cabbage fine, packed them into more jars with vinegar for sauerkraut. And Maria weaved and weaved and weaved, until the soaking barrel was empty and the stack of new baskets was as tall as Bram.

"Papa," Maria asked.

Bram marked his place in the farming book he was reading. "Ja, Schatzie?"

"May we go to Columbus tomorrow?" she asked.

Bram shook his head. "Nein. Tomorrow, I must make a lid on the well-cover. We will go soon enough."

Maria's shoulders dropped. "Yes, Papa." *But what if we don't go in time?* She wished she knew how long they had until Mr. Seymour would tire of waiting for them to leave and make good on his threat.

Laisa said, "Bram, come help me in the root cellar."

They stepped into the root cellar and shut the door. Maria sat down by Klarina, and both girls listened hard. They knew there was nothing in the root cellar Laisa couldn't get for herself. Their parents were whispering, but Maria could not make out the words.

They came out. Bram fetched a length of rope and handed it to Maria.

"What's this for?" she asked.

"Lace it through the basket handles," he said. "Tomorrow, Klarina can do your chores. You find your Pebblehoof, und you may go to Columbus to sell your baskets."

"Alone?" she asked.

Bram nodded. "Ja. You are ten years, now. Besides, you und that horse of yours have filled this house with baskets. You must carry them away."

He said it sternly, but he was smiling at her.

"Yes, Papa." Maria's heart fluttered, although she was not sure why. She had ridden Pebblehoof as far as Columbus before. She had sold baskets to Mr. LeClerc before. None of it was new, but even so the thought of doing all of it on her own filled her with a dreadful excitement.

She separated the baskets into two even stacks and laced rope through the handles, just as Bram had done before. She went to bed early, determined to make a start at morning's first light, but sleep would not come. She lay in bed, listening to the familiar sounds of family around her, until the sounds began to drift and pictures floated behind her closed eyelids.

Then the sound was of Laisa stoking up the fire for breakfast. Morning had come.

It was a chill day. The sky was the dark blue of early morning beyond the frost-touched window. Maria put on her woolen socks under her shoes and bundled her winter coat on top.

"What about breakfast, Schatzie?" Laisa asked.

"Oh, Mama. I can't wait. I'll eat when I come back for the baskets, but I best go find him now."

She set out at a slow trot, faster than walking but slow enough not to tire herself. She headed west, planning to circle around through the prairieland between the rivers, until she found them.

She ran, the crisp fall air sharp in her lungs, feeling like she could run forever. She whistled and called every so often, stopping to listen for hoofbeats.

She passed Mr. Harper's, where she saw him out front of his stable with his own riding horse. She waved, and he motioned for her to come by.

"Morning, Mr. Harper," she said when she reached him.

"Everything all right, little miss?" he asked. "Mighty early for you to be out."

"Oh, yes sir. I just need to find Pebblehoof."

"Well then, it's providential you came this way," he said. "Last evening, that herd made its way down to the river to drink, just a short piece further on."

"Truly?"

"Yes'm. The sound of 'em put my horses in quite a state, I must say. They 'bout fixed to jump out of their stalls. You hurry on, and I reckon you'll find 'em."

"I will," Maria blurted out. She ran on a dozen steps before she remembered to call back, "And thank you!"

Sure enough, not a quarter hour after she passed Mr. Harper's, she heard them. "Pebblehoof," she called out. She whistled as loud as she could manage. She crossed over one and then another prairie swell, moving towards the sound.

And then she saw him, coming straight toward her at a canter, his white blaze bright in the morning sun.

He nuzzled her shoulder and she hugged him. "Come on, boy. We've got some work, if you're game for it."

It was a pleasant ride back to the homestead. She didn't push Pebblehoof hard, not wanting to tire him out. They had a long ride yet to go, and the whole long day ahead of them for it.

When they rode into the yard, Laisa came out with a blanket in hand. The double-stack of baskets was already waiting outside the soddie's door.

Maria took the blanket and laid it over Pebblehoof's back. She stroked his neck and said, "Steady now. This is just like with the willow switches, only I'll ride too."

With Laisa's help, they arranged the blanket on Pebblehoof's back and the string of baskets evenly down each side. Maria mounted and Laisa handed up a sack. In it, Maria found a corn cake, still warm from breakfast, and a few strips of dried venison for her dinner later. Under those, she found a half-dozen carrots.

She smiled at her mother. "Thank you, Mama. I'll be back before supper."

"See you do," she said, but she was smiling too. "Und bring back a bag of salt. We are almost out."

"I will, Mama." Maria eased Pebblehoof into a walk, getting her feel. It was different with the blanket underneath her.

"Und do not take less than half a dollar each for those baskets," Laisa called after her.

"I won't." Maria waved, then set her sights to the wagon trail.

The blanket masked Pebblehoof under her. Riding him felt like trying to weave a basket with winter mittens on. She wondered how people ever rode with a saddle. The baskets swung awkwardly, too, bumping against her legs and feet.

She let Pebblehoof walk at his own speed up the trail, enjoying the chance to look on everything from up so high but at a slow enough pace she had time to see it. She ate the warm corn cake while she rode.

The prairie was brown now, the grasses dry and brittle. It was hay, as far as the eye could see, but not the sweet hay like Bram had cut when the tall grass was still green. She wondered how the herd found enough sustenance in this brown grass to live on.

The long ride was peaceful, the prairie quiet and still around her. She thought about how she used to be, back in Chicago. *I'd have thought this was passing strange, then. Me, riding bareback to do business at a prairie store.* She shook her head at the idea, and how natural it all seemed now. How nice it truly was to spend her evenings making baskets, listening to her mother tell stories of her life in Germany, or listening to her father read from the Bible.

And suddenly, she was glad. Glad to be here. Glad her parents had taken them out of Chicago. Yes, maybe Mr. Seymour would blacklist them. Maybe they wouldn't have a soul for a hundred miles to help them with anything. Maybe they would have to do for themselves. But that was fine with her. *We can do it. And it will be better than working in one of those Chicago factories,* she thought.

Yes, how much better it was to do her share for the family in a way that pleased her. *Ten whole dollars,* she thought. If she got what she wanted for the baskets, she'd go home with a stack of dollar coins tucked into her dress pocket. She reminded herself to ask her mother how long a girl would have to work in one of the factories to earn ten whole dollars.

A squabbling noise above her broke her thoughts. High above, a ragged vee of geese flew by, the birds gliding downward toward the Platte. She watched them descend until she lost them behind the trees in the bottom land.

Later, Pebblehoof spooked a family of rabbits, which burst out of hiding at the trail's edge to flee into the grass. In turn, the rabbits startled Maria. She drew in a sharp breath, only to laugh at herself.

That was the most excitement until they reached the ford over the Loup River. Maria urged Pebblehoof into the cold water. The river wasn't high with fall rains yet, but Maria lifted her feet high anyhow to avoid the splashes of Pebblehoof's strong legs.

The baskets floated on the water, then caught the current. They tugged, catching Pebblehoof unawares, and he stumbled sideways. Maria teetered, grabbing onto the rope both to hold herself and to keep the baskets under control.

"Easy, boy," she said, and she stroked his neck. She leaned him a shade to the left, pointing just up-river to account for the push of the current.

Once on the other side, Maria slid off Pebblehoof's back. She straightened the crooked blanket, and fetched a carrot out of her bag. "Good boy," she said while she fed it to him.

She walked beside him, her hand held to the rope, up from the Loup River and on into Columbus. She found Mr. Harper's mare Bessie hitched up outside of LeClerc's Dry Goods and Trading Post, and led Pebblehoof to a stop beside her.

With no one to help her, it was a sight more difficult getting the baskets off of Pebblehoof's back. Bessie watched, making Maria more aware than she liked of how awkward she must seem, but she managed.

She slung the rope's dry middle around her own neck like a yoke. She fed Pebblehoof another carrot, and said, "You stay here, now." She held up a third carrot, but did not give it to him. "You stay here and I'll give you more when I'm through."

She put the carrot back in the bag and dragged her merchandise inside.

CHAPTER 24

WHEN MARIA WENT inside, she saw Mr. LeClerc talking across the long wooden counter with two other men. One was Mr. Harper, but she did not recognize the other.

"Why, hello again, Miss Browning," Mr. Harper called out. Mr. LeClerc waved her over to the counter too.

"Bonjour, mademoiselle," said Mr. LeClerc. "You have zee bushel baskets, I see."

"Yes, sir."

"Tres bon. Wait, s'il vous plait, for a moment while I finish with zees fellows, oui?"

Maria waited while Mr. LeClerc fetched a dollar pouch of tobacco for the other man, who paid and departed.

"Zees railroad workers, zey are good for business. Now, Mr. Harper, what I can do for you?"

Mr. Harper read off a list of items he wanted before winter, most of which Mr. LeClerc said he would have to order from Omaha. He had coffee and sugar on hand and quickly packaged them up.

Mr. Harper passed a few coins across the counter, and Mr. LeClerc asked, "So, are you going to stay for zee meeting zees afternoon?"

"Indeed I will," Mr. Harper said. "It might not make two shakes of difference, but I'm sure going to tell 'em what I think about how the Union Pacific runs its business."

Maria's ears perked up. "What meeting? Is it about the railroad?"

"Yes, miss," said Mr. Harper. "Do you know, they've had the gall to tell me I have to get off my claim?"

"You too?" Maria asked. "You aren't going to do it, are you?"

"Well, now, I ain't inclined to. And I'd sure miss having such companionable neighbors."

"Oh, Mr. Harper! You can't. You can't let them run you off. We're staying. My papa decided."

"I ain't settled in my mind, yet, miss. Still, I hear they're fixing to plat a new town a few miles on down. Out by the Carters' old place. I reckon if they'd have stayed, they'd have made out right fine. If I go, maybe I'll stake a claim down there and plat into town lots."

Maria did not know what to say. She would miss Mr. Harper if he wasn't close enough to come for Sunday suppers.

He went on, "I'll give that Grenville Dodge a piece of my mind about that Mr. Seymour, then see how it shakes out."

But Maria heard only one thing. *Grenville Dodge!* "Mr. Dodge?" she asked, breathless. "Is he here?"

Mr. Harper nodded, and Mr. LeClerc said, "Oui, mademoiselle. He came yesterday afternoon, and zees morning, half zee town was outside zee depot, asking to see him. So, zees afternoon he will hold a meeting."

"Yep," Mr. Harper said. "Three o'clock, at the depot."

"My goodness! What time is it now?" Maria asked.

"I reckon about midday," Mr. Harper said.

Three hours. It wasn't much time to ride all the way home and back again with Bram. *But it's our only chance.*

"Oh Lord. Papa's been looking for Mr. Dodge all summer. I— I have to go fetch him. Mr. LeClerc, can I trust you with these baskets? I can't carry them back with me."

Mr. LeClerc nodded. "Mais oui, Cherie." He pulled the double stack of baskets by the rope, safely behind the counter. "You come again when you can, and we will do business."

"Thank you. Oh, and thank you, Mr. Harper!"

She ran outside, where Pebblehoof stood visiting with Bessie, the blanket still draped over his back. That blanket was a problem. They'd have to go fast. Pebblehoof might get too warm under it. And she didn't dare ride as fast as she needed to, with the thickness of the blanket muffling Pebblehoof's movements from her.

She snatched it off and dashed back into the store. "Will you mind these for me, too?" she asked, shoving both the blanket and her small sack of travel food into Mr. LeClerc's hands.

She ran out without waiting for an answer, taking with her only the carrot she had promised Pebblehoof. She fed it to him and mounted up. She took a deep breath, urged him into a trot, and they were off.

PEBBLEHOOF SPLASHED EASILY across the Loup River without the cumbersome baskets pulling at him in the current. Maria's legs got splashed, but she didn't care. Nothing mattered but going fast.

Once they were across the river, she leaned into him hard. "Come on, boy. We have to fly."

And fly they did. From the river bank, Pebblehoof took the slope up to the open prairie in great jolting bounds. When they

reached the top, he needed no urging to break into his full, har-
rowing gallop.

Maria had never ridden in such cold. The sting of it brought
tears to her eyes and the cold salt water burned as it dried on her
cheeks. At times her eyes watered so strongly she could scarcely
see. But she trusted Pebblehoof and could tell by the sound of his
hooves that they were on the wagon trail, not off in the rough grass.

She knew her mother would be vexed that she was returning with neither salt, nor money, nor even the blanket. But she
hoped not too awfully much. She hated to disobey, but under the
circumstances she knew she had no other choice.

Familiar landmarks passed by with such speed she could only
wonder at it. A double-hummock of ground here, a lone tree near
the trail there. She blinked the water out of her eyes once more.
Her legs began to burn with the effort of keeping her seat and she
thought, *We must be making good time.*

At last, they passed through a dip between grassy swells that
told Maria they were almost home. Bram would be there, she
knew. How quickly could he set out, she wondered.

Lost in thought, her eyes blurred with tears, she did not see
the stream bed until they were nearly upon it. When she did, her
heart leapt in her throat. They were much too close for her to
risk pulling Pebblehoof to a walk or even a trot. The stream was
low, much lower than it had been the time she fell, but she knew
Pebblehoof would jump over it anyway.

Nothing for it now but to hold on. She had only a moment to set
herself before the jump. The steady pounding of hooves on the
hard-packed trail, a sound that was such a constant presence she
had long since stopped noticing it, gave way to a sudden quiet as
they soared over the creek bed.

Pebblehoof took the landing in stride. Maria crashed down,

half to one side, barely managing to keep hold by one arm and leg, the rest of her dangling down Pebblehoof's left flank. Her other hand brushed the ground, but she did not fall.

She timed herself to the rhythm of the run, lunged up her free hand to grab a hank of Pebblehoof's black mane, and heaved herself back onto his back. Her heart thudded in her chest and her eyes were opened wide in spite of the cold wind.

Home was close now. She let Pebblehoof run full for another minute, then eased him back off the gallop as the soddie came into view.

"Papa!" She screamed full voice as they came onto the homestead. "Papa, it's Mr. Dodge!" She didn't see him, straight off, but knew he had to be somewhere close.

Both Bram and Laisa came bursting out of the soddie as Maria rode into the yard.

"Mein lieber Scholli!" Bram said. His rifle was in his hands. "What is it?"

Laisa said, "Schatzie! Are you all right? Und where is the salt? Und the blanket?"

"Oh, hang the blanket, Mama! Scold me later if you must but never mind that now! He's here, Papa. He's in Columbus right now!"

"Who is here?"

"That railroad man, Mr. Dodge! He came. There's to be a meeting today." Laisa's hand shot up to her mouth. Maria went on, words tumbling out of her between panting gulps of air, "Mr. Harper told me, and he'll be there too. It's at three o'clock at the depot, and everybody's going to be there. Oh, you have to go, Papa! Hurry!"

"Grenville Dodge?" Bram asked. His jaw hung loose. "All right. Calm yourself, und tell me again from the beginning."

She slid off of Pebblehoof's back and recounted, as best she could, what Mr. LeClerc and Mr. Harper had told her. When she finished, she said, "It's our only chance, Papa. You have to go."

Laisa held up a hand to silence her. "It is your father's decision, Schatzie." She turned to her husband. "What will you do, Bram?"

Bram looked down at his shoes. "Och. I am a fool for my temper. After last time, who will believe me? Dodge is ein wichtiger railroad man, und Mr. Seymour will only say I tried to shoot him. Then we are as good as blacklisted anyway."

Maria looked at her mother. It was plain on her face she wanted to scold Bram about that. None of it was fair, and especially that blacklist. But what if they stayed on their claim and refused to let the railroad men cross it? They would always be poor, and Papa would never have his own print shop. *But we could stay, couldn't we?* Maria wondered.

Perhaps. But, she realized, perhaps not. Chicago had policemen to keep the peace. But on the prairie there was no one. Once they were blacklisted, with not a soul to help them, Mr. Seymour's men could come again at any time to make mischief or worse.

Klarina was watching from the doorway now. *Who would protect her,* Maria wondered, *if anything happened?*

"You say we can stay, Papa, even with the blacklist. But that's not true. It's not! Those men might come back any time and there won't be anybody for miles who might help us. They could steal Poppy and Reine. Or steal our winter stores, or burn up the wood pile, or salt the well. Anything."

Her parents both looked at her, shocked at her boldness, as she continued. "We can't stay with that blacklist. They'll drive us off anyway, Papa, you know they will. And I don't want to leave! I like it here. I didn't always, but I do now. You have to go talk to Mr. Dodge. Please, Papa, I don't want to leave."

"Want?" Bram yelled. "What has *want* to do with anything? I did not want to leave Mainz, Schatzie, but I had to! I am the father, und blacklist or no, we will do as I say!"

Maria leaned into Pebblehoof. Her eyes welled up with tears that had nothing to do with the cold. She knew she should keep quiet. It wasn't her place to speak out. But everything was falling apart. First the Carters — who she hadn't even known — had left. Bram was wrong. Soon enough, they'd have to leave too, with no choice but to make for Chicago. She thought again. There was no reason to keep quiet. *There isn't anything left to lose.* It was a bleak, gray thought, but it gave her a spark of courage.

"You won't be alone, Papa. Mr. Harper will be there. Everybody'll be there. Nobody likes that old Mr. Seymour."

Bram shook his head slightly. "I do not know. If only I had not shot his fool hat off." He flung the rifle away from himself. Laisa and Maria cringed, but the rifle clattered harmlessly to the ground next to the canvas woodshed.

All was silent again, except for the steady whoosh of Pebblehoof's breath.

Then Maria's mother spoke. "This is the same as in Deutschland. We came to this land for freedom, Bram. Unsere Freiheit! But this does not mean we must not also fight for it."

Bram took a deep breath, and blew out a cloud of steam. He stepped to Laisa's side, put his arm around her shoulders, and kissed her temple.

"Ja. You are right, Liebchen. I must try, anyway. By Gott, I will try. But it is a long ride. I do not know if Poppy can go in time."

But I can, Maria thought. "Pebblehoof can take you, Papa. He'll carry you. If I'm with you, I know he will. He's fast and strong. We'll make it."

Bram looked up at Pebblehoof. "I have never ridden bareback," he said. Maria smiled as she threw herself back up onto Pebblehoof's shoulders.

"It's easy, Papa. You'll like it."

"Wait," he said. "I must get the claim papers." He ran inside, and came out a moment later. Maria held a hand down to him and he took it. He jumped, Maria pulled, and he flopped clumsily onto Pebblehoof's back behind his daughter.

Maria leaned forward. "Come on, boy," she said, and off they went.

But Pebblehoof was tired, and with Bram's weight he would not gallop. She urged him into a jolting, bouncing canter, but he would go no faster. She thought they were making half the speed as before, perhaps, but no more.

"I hope the meeting starts late," she said.

"Ja," Bram agreed. Then he said, "It is gut you will be there also. I will need you to say what those men did to your mama."

Maria swallowed. "Must I? Can't you do it?"

"Nein. I was not there. I did not see what happened like you did."

Maria hoped never to see those men again. She almost couldn't bear the thought of calling them out in front of everyone. Almost. But if it helped somehow to sway Mr. Dodge's good opinion, she would do it.

"All right, Papa. I will."

CHAPTER 25

T HE STREETS OF Columbus were deserted. Even Mr. LeClerc's store was closed up. They rode down Main Street and turned towards the railroad depot. The building had grown, now standing tall with clapboard siding rising up over the low stone foundations.

They could hear the sound of voices inside from a block away.

"Hurry," Bram said. "Already they have started."

They dismounted outside the depot, where several other horses were hitched to a wooden rail.

"Thank you, Pebblehoof," Maria said. "I know you're tired. If this works, we'll have you to thank for it."

"Come, Maria," Bram said, and they went in.

Inside, the depot was a muddle of people sitting on makeshift clapboard benches, practically filling the whole space. It seemed everyone was talking to his neighbor, but it also seemed that the meeting had not quite started after all.

The depot was little more than a large empty room, its high roof held up by poles running down the middle. Glass windows dotted the walls, and the inside was the bright yellow of new pine. At one end was an empty space with no benches where Maria saw four men standing. Two were the roughs who had hurt her mother. The third was Silas Seymour.

The fourth man she did not recognize. *That must be Mr. Dodge.* He was thin. He stood erect in a blue army uniform, a double row of shiny brass buttons down its front. His face was thin to match his frame, with a full but neatly-trimmed beard and moustache. His skin was nut-brown with sunshine.

All the benches near the front were filled, but towards the back there were still seats. Bram held Maria's hand and led her through the crowd, where they found an empty space next to Mr. Harper.

"I'm glad to see you, Mr. Harper," said Maria.

"You too, Miss Browning." But as he turned to look at her, she saw a fresh bruise on his cheek.

"Oh, what happened?" she asked, motioning towards his face. "That wasn't there this morning."

Mr. Harper just shook his head. "It don't matter." There was also a gap in his teeth where none had been before.

"Did they do that to you?" She tipped her head towards the front of the room.

"I said it don't matter." Mr. Harper rubbed at his ribs.

Bram said, "Maria says you will speak, ja?"

Mr. Harper shook his head. "No sir. I was set to, but not now," he answered. "I stayed in town, so I reckon I may as well come to the meeting, but no. You speak up for yourselves if you've a mind to, but I ain't gon' speak. The wind blows where it will, and a man cain't do no good blowing against it."

Bram gave Maria a stern look. She wondered how many other people in the room were in the same situation. *And how many of them has Mr. Seymour already scared off?* Like that Mr. and Mrs. Carter who left for Fort Kearny. She prayed someone else would speak up too.

Bram leaned down to whisper in Maria's ear. "I think we are on our own."

Maria's heart, which was still beating fast from the ride, quickened its pace again. When she told what had happened to her mother, she would have to make it good. *And in front of such a crowd!* She had not imagined so very many people.

"Attention!" a voice from the front barked out. Everyone turned towards Mr. Dodge

"I call this meeting to order," he said. "For those who don't know me, I'm Major General Grenville M. Dodge of the Federal Army, retired, and presently chief engineer of the Union Pacific Railroad company. I understand a number of you have matters of business you wish to take up with the Union Pacific. We will take you all in turn, but I will have an orderly meeting, is that clear?"

No one objected.

"Very well." He glanced at a sheet of paper. "The chair recognizes Mr. Stuart Lassen. Stand and state your business."

A man rose, saying he hadn't been paid for the lumber of the very building they were all in. Mr. Dodge told him to bring his contract to the railroad office the next morning.

One by one, Mr. Dodge called on the people whose names were on the paper. One fellow wanted payment for the food he supplied to the workers at the depot.

Mr. Dodge called out, "Who else is here for want of payments?" A number of hands shot up. Mr. Dodge turned to Mr. Seymour. "It seems you've been lax in your bookkeeping, Silas."

A few people laughed, but not many, and Mr. Dodge quickly quieted them down.

"You folks come to the office tomorrow morning with Mr. Lassen, and we'll get you sorted out." He asked those people's names and crossed them off the list.

"Papa, we're not on his list," Maria said. "What will we do?"

"I don't know. Just keep quiet, Schatzie."

Maria thought a moment. *We have to get on that list!* But she did not want to interrupt the meeting. Then she had an idea.

She leaned towards Mr. Harper and said, "Are you on the list?" He nodded that he was.

"Please, sir," she whispered, "may we speak in your place?"

"You sure about that?" he asked.

"Yes sir. We have to try."

Mr. Harper gave her a sober look, but he nodded his head.

"Thank you," she said. She was relieved, but could scarcely pay attention to the rest of the meeting. Her stomach flipped end over end with the thought of speaking up against Mr. Seymour, and to such a powerful man as Mr. Dodge. *What if he doesn't believe us?*

At last, she heard Mr. Dodge call, "Mr. Harper, stand and state your business."

Mr. Harper stood up. "Thank you, sir. With all due respect, I have decided not to speak." Maria caught a small sneer flicker across Mr. Seymour's face. "However, I would ask to give my time to my neighbors, the Brownings."

Mr. Dodge shrugged, and made a note on his list. "Very well. Brownings, stand and state your business."

Bram stood, holding his hat in front of him. Maria stood with him.

Bram said, "I remember you, Mr. Dodge, from one year ago. We had an arrangement for five acres from the corner of my claim. But now Mr. Seymour, he moves the railroad line, to cut in half my land—"

Mr. Dodge held up a hand, and Bram paused. "Moved the line? I am aware of no such move. How do you know this?"

"Because we had an arrangement for five acres, not eighty! Und when I tell him I will not leave, he tries to force us off. He burned my wheat crop, und hurt my wife, even."

"I did no such thing," Mr. Seymour interjected.

"Order, Silas," Dodge said. "Mr. Browning, those are serious claims. Do you have any proof? Did you see him set the fire?"

Bram looked downward. "Nein. We did not see who it was."

"That's unfortunate," said Mr. Dodge, but it didn't sound like he really thought so.

Bram's fingers curled around the brim of his hat, crushing it. Though the room was not warm, Maria saw a sheen of sweat on his forehead. "But who else could it be?" he said. "Und my wife, she almost died!"

"In the fire?"

"Nein, that was before. With the soap, when I was here to talk to you."

"Soap?" Mr. Dodge asked. "Talking to me? Sir, you are making little sense. I haven't been in Columbus since I made the survey."

"Och, I—" Bram faltered, his lips hanging slightly apart.

Maria's heart beat faster than ever. *It's not working.* For all she dreaded speaking to this powerful man, Maria never imagined her father might balk at it too. *I have to say something.*

Maria tugged at his sleeve. Bram looked at her, panic plain on his face. Then he said, "My daughter. She has better English. She saw. She can say."

Mr. Dodge said, "Go ahead, miss."

Maria swallowed down the lump in her throat. *It's all up to me.* She took a deep breath and began.

"Thank you, sir. Like Papa said, somebody did set fire to our crops. But that was after. He means Mama was burned before that. He came here to look for you, sir, because Mr. Seymour wants to run the line through our claim. We were making soap that same day, my mama and sister and me, when two men rode up."

She told what had happened, what she had seen, what she had heard from inside the soddie, and what she found when she came back outside.

"And Mama was on the ground, crying out something awful." Her voice quavered and caught in her throat, but she knew she must go on. "The soap was spilled all over her arm, and the men were riding away."

"That's all lies!" Mr. Seymour shouted. "My boys never hurt nobody."

"They did," Maria repeated.

"I don't know, Mr. Browning," Dodge said. "It would seem to be you and your daughter's word against his. This wouldn't be the first time someone used a sad story to squeeze a dollar out of the Union Pacific Railroad."

Maria felt her eyes well up, and fought the tears back. "But they did! It was those two," she pointed at the rough men standing with Mr. Seymour.

"Well then where is this burned woman?" Mr. Seymour demanded. "Why didn't she come this evening? I'll tell you why. 'Cause it never happened, that's why!"

Maria didn't know what to do. *What else can I say?* Then a white haired man across the room stood up. Doc Hastings.

"You are out of order, sir," said Mr. Dodge.

"I apologize, but I'm the doctor here and I can confirm that it did indeed happen. I treated Mrs. Browning myself, and it was an awful, awful burn. It was a miracle she did not lose the arm."

Mr. Seymour gave a derisive snort. "Well, what of it? Apparently there's no harm done."

"No harm?" Doc shot back. "No harm, sir? The poor woman suffered for weeks, and you call it no harm? I know what I saw, Seymour, and you wouldn't call it no harm had it been your arm."

The crowd grumbled. Doc Hastings smiled at Maria, and gave her a quick wink as he sat down.

"That don't prove my boys did it," Mr. Seymour said. He pointed at Maria. "It's just her word how it happened. You boys didn't hurt Mrs. Browning, did you?" The roughs shook their heads. "I reckon Mrs. Browning just took a wrong step or some such thing, and knocked the kettle over herself."

"Oh, no sir!" Maria said, her voice almost in a shout. "I heard a gun go off. I don't think they meant to hurt anybody, because I heard one of them yell to the other that they weren't supposed to, but they did. A bullet hit the top of the cook stand and broke it. That's how the pot spilled."

"You can't believe that," Mr. Seymour said. "Besides, that crazy Hessian plum near killed me. Shot the hat right off my head!"

"Pipe down, Mr. Seymour," said Mr. Dodge. "Miss Browning has the floor. Is that true, miss?"

"Yes, sir, but that was after Mama was burned. Mr. Seymour came back and tried to give Papa two hundred and fifty dollars for our claim."

A murmur rippled through the crowd. Someone said, "Highway robbery!"

Mr. Dodge shouted for order. He gave a sideways look towards Mr. Seymour. "Two hundred and fifty for an improved claim? In that case, Silas, I scarcely blame him," said Mr. Dodge. "Sounds to me like your boys did burn that woman. You're lucky he only shot your hat."

Dodge turned back to Bram. "Mr. Browning, I am very sorry to hear about your wife's injury and the Union Pacific will certainly make restitution for Doctor Hastings' services. Miss Browning, do you know which one of them did it?"

The whole room was looking at her. Mr. Seymour, with venom to spare. But Doc Hastings had a smile in his eyes, and others gave looks that offered some kind of hope.

She nodded. "Whichever one's Delbert. He's the one who hurt my mama. I'm sorry I don't know his family name."

"Is that all, Miss Browning?" Mr. Dodge asked.

Maria paused. She wanted nothing more than to be finished. To sit down and get everyone's eyes off of her. But she couldn't. She thought of Mr. Harper bringing her home, fixing Poppy's hoof, and even giving them this chance to speak.

Another memory came to her about Mr. Harper. It was something she hadn't thought about since it happened, not since that terrible day her mother was burned. Mr. Harper and Mr. Seymour, talking outside the railroad office. Mr. Harper's back against the wall and the look on Mr. Seymour's face when he had told her to go away.

She saw Mr. Harper gingerly probe the bruise on his face with the tips of his fingers. *He's going to leave too.* She couldn't bear it. What if Poppy got hurt again? Or Pebblehoof? She took a deep breath.

"Well, no. That's not all," she said. "I'm sorry to speak for you, Mr. Harper, but you saved Poppy and I have to say something even if you won't."

She turned back to Mr. Dodge. "They're doing the same to him, pushing him off his claim. When I came to Columbus to fetch Doc Hastings, I saw Mr. Seymour threatening Mr. Harper outside the railroad office. Now he's got a shiner fresh as warm milk and a tooth gone what was there when I saw him earlier.

He won't say it but I know he's going to leave, too. They already got the Carters to leave, who had a claim down a piece from Mr. Harper's. It's not right, sir. It's just not right."

"Carter," Mr. Dodge said. "Yes. I remember them. They were right nice folks. Put me up for two nights last fall when it was raining so's I wished I had an ark." He shot a glance at Mr. Seymour and his boys. "No. If this is all true, then it isn't right. Not at all. Mr. Harper? What say you?"

Mr. Harper winced as he stood. He took a shallow, pained breath. "Yes, sir. It's true. Every word of it." His voice whistled oddly through the new gap in his teeth.

"Why didn't you say something?" Mr. Dodge asked.

"Well sir, Mr. Seymour's boys come to me in town this afternoon to give me this," he touched his fingers gingerly to his swollen cheek, "and they told me if I opened my mouth tonight I'd be saying my last words. I'm plum shamed to admit they cowed me, sir. Shamed. But if this young lady can stand up for me, then by God I can stand up for myself."

He marched to the front of the room to face Silas directly, arms outstretched. "Mr. Seymour, if you want to plug me dead here in front of everybody, you go right ahead. I came west to live free, and I'd rather be dead than let the likes of you bully me around one more minute. But you do it your own self. Don't be hidin' behind those thugs of yours."

A chorus of voices rose up from the crowd, shouts of, "He's been after me too!" and, "He's a crook."

"Order!" Mr. Dodge hollered, and the crowd obeyed. He held up a hand for silence, then said, "All right. Mr. Browning, I accept your claims against Mr. Seymour and his men, and I will deal with them."

"What?" Mr. Seymour burst out. "You can't believe all this

claptrap, Grenville! These folks are just standing in the way of progress, that's all."

"I said pipe down, Silas, or this crowd'll be out for blood! If they're not already. Mr. Harper, I take it you are in largely the same situation as the Brownings. Will you also agree to whatever resolution is acceptable to them?"

"I will," said Mr. Harper, and he returned to stand by Maria's side.

"Very well. Then Mr. Browning, what is it you ask of me?"

Bram cleared his throat. "I want the railroad moved to your original line. You are a decent man, und I will honor our agreement for five of my acres. But I have a proper claim, filed with the land office in Omaha, und marked out just as required by the Homestead Act. I want a paper, signed by your hand, that my land will be left alone."

"You said some crops were burned, I believe. Are you asking restitution for those?" Mr. Dodge asked.

Bram considered, then shook his head. "Nein. They were small fields anyhow. I only want to work my land in peace."

There was silence for a moment, while Mr. Dodge considered. Then Bram went on. "Wait. There is one other thing. I would know *why*. Why does Mr. Seymour want to move the line? Why does he cause all this trouble? This, I do not understand."

"I reckon I'm quite curious on that account myself," said Mr. Dodge. "Mr. Seymour, what have you to say? Why would you want to run these honest, hardworking homesteaders off their land? And more to it, what gives you the right to go breaking agreements I've made and move my railroad line?"

Mr. Seymour stammered, "Well, I, it wasn't like that."

A new voice joined in. "I can answer you, sir." A stout-looking man stood at one of the front benches. "If I may have the floor."

"Papa," Maria whispered. "Who's that?"

"It is Mr. Train. Quiet, now."

"He's out of order," Seymour fairly shouted, his face burning so red Maria thought he might just burst into flame.

"Mr. Seymour is correct," said Mr. Dodge, "You're George Train, is that right? You are out of order, sir. But as Mr. Seymour seems so ill inclined to let you speak, I should like to hear what you have to say. The floor is yours."

Mr. Train began. "Thank you, sir. These folks," he swept his hand toward the crowd, "are only guilty of standing in the way of Mr. Seymour's pocketbook, not progress. He's in league with that bed-weevil boss of yours, Mr. Durant. They want to build a shorter track than yours, requiring less of the money Congress has allocated. I reckon it a trifling mystery into whose pockets they would have the excess go. Why, Mr. Seymour himself has already bought up some five thousand dollars' worth of lots here in Columbus, and on credit. I for one can see no other way for him to make good those debts, unless you're paying a handsomer wage than I'd expect."

Dodge rounded on Mr. Seymour. "Is that true? Did you go behind my back to Mr. Durant with this, you crooked snake?"

"I did no such thing!" said Mr. Seymour. "It was Durant's idea, and he's the boss."

"No, sir." Mr. Dodge said. He stood up to his full height. "I marked out the line! I surveyed the best route, with the fewest cuts and fills and on the gentlest grade. Mr. Durant may own this railroad, but I am still the chief engineer and the line goes where I say."

"But—" Mr. Seymour started.

"Don't you say another word," Mr. Dodge ordered. "Any fool can see this town doesn't think kindly of you. You move my railroad without so much as a by-your-leave. You make a liar out of me, ignoring agreements I've made with Mr. Browning and everybody else in this town by the sound of it. And you have the arrogant gall to threaten honest homesteaders? Your boys hurt a woman, for the love of God, and don't think that doesn't fall on your shoulders too. If I was the sheriff, I'd arrest you. But I ain't, so all I can do is tell you you're fired, you hear? Fired! And your boys, there, with you."

Mr. Seymour's jaw dropped, but he made no retort.

Mr. Dodge reached inside his coat and pulled out a bill fold. He drew out a stack of paper money and counted some out in quick, sharp motions. "Here's your month's pay," he said. "I'll hold back twenty dollars for the Brownings' medical expenses."

"Twenty dollars! Why, I—"

"Be glad it's not more," Mr. Dodge yelled directly into Mr. Seymour's face, pushing the thin stack of money to Mr. Seymour's chest. "Now I suggest you and your rats head out of town while I conclude business with these fine people. I hate to think what might happen if you were sluggish in your departure."

Mr. Seymour clenched his jaw so hard Maria heard the squeak of his teeth from the back of the room. His face flushed to crimson and he glared into Mr. Dodge's unyielding eyes, but all he said was, "Come on, boys."

Everyone rose to their feet as Mr. Seymour and his henchmen left, then the meeting dissolved into a chaos of cheers. People clapped Bram on the back and told Maria what a brave girl she was.

Mr. Dodge brought the crowd to order. "Mr. Browning," he announced, "I accept your terms."

The crowd cheered again. Bram swept Maria up into a great hug and over the din of the crowd she just heard him say, "I am proud of you, Schatzie. Danke."

Maria smiled so wide her cheeks hurt. *And you'll get your print shop, too,* she thought. *I promised I'd help you.*

This time, Mr. Dodge did not call for order. When the crowd settled itself down, Mr. Dodge assured everyone he would stay in Columbus for the rest of the season to see the railroad laid where he originally indicated. He gave Bram the twenty dollars, plus fifty more for the five acres. He even wrote out and signed a promise for Bram, right then and there, that the Union Pacific Railroad would not stray so much as one inch beyond them.

He made out another paper for Mr. Harper, and it was over.

Mr. Harper took his hat off and crouched down until he was eye to eye with Maria.

"I'm much obliged to you, young lady," he said. "You folks are the finest neighbors a man could wish for."

"So you'll stay?" Maria asked.

"Why, sure I'll stay." He smiled broad. "Where else should I want to be? It's a fine country for horses."

CHAPTER 26

THE FULL BLUSH of evening graced the skies as they left the depot. Most of the horses that had been hitched outside were gone. So was Pebblehoof.

Maria whistled and called for him. She looked all around the building, but he was not there.

"Where could he be?" she asked.

Bram shrugged. "I do not know. Let us finish our business with Mr. LeClerc, und we will search for him."

"Oh, Papa, you don't think Mr. Seymour and his men— I mean, he was pretty mad. Maybe they—" But she couldn't finish the thought.

"Perhaps. But nein, I do not think so. Perhaps he has only gone to the river for water."

That must be it, she thought. *He's down at the river.*

The dry goods store was crowded when they entered, filled with people catching up their afternoon business. The place crackled with a glad air. Several people cheered and clapped when Maria and Bram came in.

Maria blushed so hard she thought her ears might catch fire. Folks came up to shake their hands, most of whom Maria didn't even know. Mr. LeClerc was so happy about finally getting his money from the railroad that he gave Maria an extra nickel for every bushel basket.

"Have no worries for me," he said. "I will have no trouble selling zees baskets, when people learn you have made them. You are famous, cherie! Zee girl who beat Silas Seymour." He laughed and the crowd laughed with him, but it was all right because everyone was happy.

They departed with pockets full of money, a bag of salt, and the blanket Maria had left in Mr. LeClerc's care.

Maria whistled and called for Pebblehoof as they walked down to the Loup River, but he did not come. In the silty ground at the river's edge she found tracks that must have been his, the prints of a horse with no shoes. But darkness was falling quickly and they were hard to see.

"He must have crossed over," Maria said.

Bram nodded. "Ja. Und we must make our own way across too."

Bram held tight to Maria's hand as they stepped into the river. The frigid water shocked Maria's ankles, and shocked her again with every step until she was soaked up to her ribs. She held the blanket in a roll above her head, while Bram carried the salt on one shoulder.

Maria tried calling again when they reached the other side, but she was shivering so much she could scarcely make a sound or whistle at all.

Bram wrapped the blanket around her. Through chattering teeth, he said, "Do not worry, Schatzie. Surely he has only gone back to his herd."

Maria nodded. *I hope so*, she prayed.

"Come," Bram said. "It is a long way home, und we must bring your mother und sister the good news."

They walked quickly to keep from freezing as the chill of night descended.

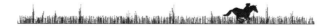

OCTOBER PRESSED ON toward All Hallows Eve. Frost became a regular morning sight. At first, the frost vanished by midday. Then it clung to the shadows, vanishing only where the sun reached. As the days passed, it stayed on the ground in defiance of the sun.

On all of these days, Maria looked for Pebblehoof. She scoured the wedge of prairie between the two rivers, from north to south, and farther east and west than she had ever walked, but she did not find him. She returned home, glum and sober, her hands and cheeks pink with the cold.

One day, she stopped at Mr. Harper's.

"I can't find him anymore," she said. "I'm worried."

"'Bout what?"

"That somebody might've taken him from outside the depot that day. Or maybe Mr. Seymour's men did something to him."

"Now don't you fret," said Mr. Harper. "You never had a bridle on that horse, did you?"

Maria shook her head.

"Then I don't reckon he stayed outside that depot, with all the hollering ruckus going on inside. I'd wager a jar of your mother's blackberry preserves he was long gone before Seymour and his boys ever set foot outside."

Maria thought about it. After all, why would Pebblehoof have stayed? She sighed. "I suppose so."

"He's with his herd, or I don't know a hoof from a hindquarter. The grass is all dry and dead 'round here. I expect they've moved on, now that the weather runs cold."

"Do you think they'll be back in the spring?"

"I cain't rightly say. Could be, but only the good Lord knows."

After that, she prayed on it often.

ANOTHER MORNING, LAISA sent her out for coneflower roots. She handed Maria a basket and the small metal trowel. "As many as you can. Before the ground is too frozen for digging."

Maria bundled up under an extra blouse and shawl, wishing her father had found the time to make those rabbit fur boots. She knew those would not likely come until Christmas.

The pale autumn sun glared low in the east, so Maria took the trail west. Her breath hung in clouds, lazy in the still air. She knew she might find coneflower easily, if she went into the grass, but she was not eager for it. It was warmer to walk than to freeze her fingers in the frigid soil. If she went far enough, she reckoned, she would come upon some by the trail.

She passed the Carters' old claim before she came to any, a thick patch of coneflower plants in a shady hollow near a frozen stream. She set down the basket and knelt to dig.

The ground was hard, and she worked as the sun moved full south. She put her back to it, drawing from it a little warmth.

A low wind came in gusts now and then, first this way, then that. Except for her own breathing and the sound of the trowel scraping the soil, all was stillness. The birds had all gone. Insects were hidden away in their secret winter homes. For a moment, Maria had the feeling she was the only living thing on the whole of the Nebraska prairie.

Then a gust came, bringing with it a sound that was not her own. A faint, low rumbling that triggered a memory. The sky was blue over distant haze, but there was not a cloud in it.

Not thunder. Is it— Did she dare hope? She did. She dropped the trowel in the basket and dashed up to the high ground above the frozen stream.

She closed her eyes, listening, putting her whole self into the world of sound. The air shifted and she heard it again from the west.

Before she knew what she was doing, she was sprinting into the dry grass. "Pebblehoof!" she shouted. "Pebblehoof!"

She whistled and called, running toward the sound. She tripped on the backside of a gentle hill, sprawling on her stomach. She rose and kept on, the waves of ground passing under her until her legs quivered with effort, her head grew light, and her lungs wheezed with the cold. But still, she could not see them.

She stopped to listen, struggling to keep her dry throat from coughing. They were out there, somewhere. *If only I can get close enough.*

She ran on, ten minutes more, then twenty, feeling herself slowing with each grassy hummock she crossed. She fought her way to the top of one last rise, but could not go on. "Pebblehoof," she called, one more time, before giving in to a fit of coughs and wheezes.

She fell to her knees, panting, crying, and then sank down fully onto the ground. *I'll never see him again.*

She lay there, feeling the heat of her body bleed out into the frozen ground beneath her. She knew she must get up. She must finish her chore and return home. But not now. For that moment, she didn't care if she ever rose again.

Then she heard hoofbeats. Not the rumble of many but the clear, triple-beat of one horse at the canter. *It's him!* She jumped to her feet.

And it was.

All the tiredness vanished from her limbs. She ran, meeting him in the middle. She lashed her arms around his neck, burying her nose in his coat. He nickered at her, his warmth enveloping her.

"We did it, Pebblehoof. We don't have to go back to Chicago, and Papa's going to have his print shop in a year or two, he says. Thank you. I couldn't have done it without you."

She hugged him for a long while, until her hands and cheeks pressed against him were no longer cold.

"I missed you, boy." She stroked the velvet of his nose, and scratched under his mane. She knew horses didn't smile, but it almost looked like he was. *Or maybe I'm smiling big enough for the both of us*, she thought.

"Come on," she said. She mounted up. From her high seat she saw the herd in the distance, moving away south. Dust rose up behind them. "Let's ride!"

Pebblehoof turned towards the herd. Maria didn't care. Anywhere was fine, so long as they were together. She slipped into the glassy rhythm of his gallop. Her bonnet blew back off her head, hanging by its laces behind her. Her hair whipped wild.

They caught up with the herd, briefly joining their sound to the herd's thunder, then left the herd behind. They raced on, into lands Maria had never set eyes on. She floated in a joy she hoped Pebblehoof shared even half so much as her.

She wanted to go on. To stay with him. To stay with the herd, learn to eat grass, to live wild and free.

But I cannot. They were so far west, she knew they must be close to Pawnee land. Perhaps they were in it already.

She eased him back around, slowed him to a trot, and rode until once more they found the herd. Maria dismounted. She kissed his muscular jaw and blinked away her tears.

Her heart caught in her throat. "You come back in the spring, you hear?"

Pebblehoof neighed at her and tossed his head. His eyes blinked, his long, black lashes waving her goodbye, and he trotted away with the herd.

Maria watched them go. She stood with her arm held high, waving, until the herd vanished over the hills.

Her arm dropped. Her mother would scold her about losing another basket, but she didn't mind. She could make another one. She wiped the wetness from her cheeks and began the long walk home.

GLOSSARY

A LIST OF German words and phrases used in this book:

Ach	Ah, an interjection
Alles	All, or everything
Arbeitspferd	A work horse
Auf Wiedersehen	Goodbye
Baumstark	As strong as a horse
Bin	Am
Bitte sehr	You're welcome
Danke	Thank you
Deutschland	Germany
Die	The
Drecksack	A swear word
Ein	A / an
Er	He
Fieser	An obnoxious person
Freiheit	Freedom.
Für	For
Gehst hinein	Get inside.
Gehen	Go
Gut / gute / gutes	Good
Gott	God
Grunddeinstbarkeit	Easement; a right to use a section of land
Herr	Mister
Ich	I
Ist	Is

Ja	Yes (pronounced as "ya")
Kleine Maus	Little Mouse, a nickname
Kultur zu erschaffen	To create culture
Lassen	Let, as in "let us alone"
Liebchen, Lieben	Dear, or darling
Mädchen	Girl or girls
Mainz	A city in Germany
Mann	Husband
Mein, Meine	My
Mein lieber Scholli	My goodness!
Mit	With
Nein	No
Nicht, nichts	Nothing
Och	Oh, an interjection
Pferd	Horse
Ruhe	Peace
Schatzi	Honey or sweetheart, as a nickname
Schliesst	To block, as in "block the door"
Sehr gut	Very good
Sehr wohl	Very well, as in agreeing to something
Sie	You
Sprechen	Speak
Teufelsmensch	Devil-man, an epithet
Teufelspferd	Demon horse
Tür	Door
Und	And
Uns	Us
Unsere	Our
Verbrüht	Scalded; burned
Verstehst du?	Do you understand?
Wichtiger	Important
Wieder	Again

AUTHOR'S NOTE

IT HAS BEEN a delight for me to write this book. But I found the research for it was almost as much fun as the writing. Studying up on frontier life for families taking advantage of the new Homestead Act of 1862 taught me a lot of very interesting things about American history.

In writing a historical novel, one must always balance true history with the made-up story one wants to tell. In this novel I have tried to be as true to the history as I could, while inventing only what was necessary for the story. Here, I want to separate fiction from fact. Facts are important, and true history has its own story to tell.

REAL PEOPLE

THERE ARE FOUR people in this story who were real historical figures. Within the story I have tried to stay true to each man's character, as best as I understand it. In this note, I want to do more than I could within the novel to share a bit of who these men were.

The first is Thomas C. Durant, one of the controlling partners of the Union Pacific Railroad company. As far as I can tell, he was not a nice man. Although he was not officially in charge of the Union Pacific's operations, through a variety of shady, back-room maneuvers, he was the man calling the shots. Further, he was never one to shy away from

Thomas C. Durant

lining his pockets. Indeed, he made one of his earlier fortunes by manipulating the stock market in ways that, if he were caught doing it today, would land him in jail.

In a curious quirk of history, Durant once hired Abraham Lincoln, when Lincoln was a private practice attorney, to defend him in a lawsuit. This association proved very profitable later, when President Lincoln selected Durant's Union Pacific company to build the eastern section of the Transcontinental Railroad.

The second man is Major General Grenville M. Dodge. Dodge got his start as a surveyor, without which he would surely not have ended up in this book. He studied civil engineering in college before engaging in a career as a surveyor for the decade leading up to the Civil War.

Dodge joined the Union Army at the start of the war. He was twice wounded in combat; once while leading the Union troops in the Battle of Pea Ridge, in Arkansas, then a second time during the siege of Atlanta, Georgia.

Dodge's association with Thomas Durant began during the war, where his information enabled Durant to

Maj. Gen. Grenville M. Dodge

smuggle cotton out of the South. Durant made a fortune this way, although it is not clear whether Dodge profited as well.

Later, Durant hired Dodge as the Union Pacific's chief engineer, to survey the route the railroad would take and to oversee construction of it. Despite Dodge's abetting of smuggling activities during the war, he seems to have been a basically honorable fellow. This quality brought him into frequent opposition with Durant.

Thomas Durant owned considerable land holdings throughout the west. That land would become much more valuable if a railroad somehow happened to pass through it. Durant thus placed considerable pressure on Grenville Dodge to have the line follow a route that would most improve the value of Durant's land. Grenville Dodge, being an engineer, wanted the railroad to take what he saw as the most sensible route.

The two did not always agree, and eventually Thomas Durant hired a consulting engineer to work under Dodge. This junior engineer was not there to help Dodge, however, but to spy on him for Mr. Durant.

The consulting engineer was the third man, named Silas Seymour. Today, very little is known about Mr. Seymour. He was born in 1817 in Stillwater, New York. He married a woman who, by complete and unexpected coincidence, shares a name with my daughter.

Silas Seymour, seated at left.

Seymour worked his way up through a number of smaller, regional railroads in the eastern United States, eventually becoming the chief engineer of the Buffalo and New York City Railroad. Later, he built a bridge across the Potomac River for a railroad near Washington, D.C. It is thus that his skill at bridge building plays a small part in this story.

I do not know Silas Seymour's personal views on slavery, but he did write a letter at the start of the Civil War supporting the institution of slavery in the South, and believed that the southern states should have a separate government from the North. Other than that, he seems to have had very little to do with the war, which raged in the years leading up to and including the start of this novel.

At any rate, his position as a spy for Thomas Durant made him the ideal figure to serve as this story's villain. In that light I have cast him as a sinister fellow, with apologies to his heirs for the memory of their ancestor.

The fourth man was George F. Train, who was not a railroad man despite his name. That his name was Train strikes me as one of the stranger coincidences in this novel. George Train was a hotel man and a banker. He was also something of a visionary, even though his grandest dream never came to pass.

George Train envisioned a chain of glorious cities, from east to west, along the route of the Transcontinental Railroad. Chief among them, in his mind, was Columbus, Nebraska. In later years, when the nearby town of Cleveland gained a hotel, Mr. Train took this as such a threat to Columbus's prominence that he bought the hotel and moved it to Columbus.

George Francis Train

Mr. Train ardently promoted the town of Columbus. He believed the nation's capital should be near the geographical center of the United States. To him, the most sensible choice was Columbus. He often billed the town, in his own words, as "the new center of the Union and quite probably the future capital of the U.S.A."

George Train owned a lot of land in Columbus, and given his position as the town's leading figure, he seemed the appropriate person in this novel to finally reveal the reasons behind Durant and Seymour's sinister plot against the homesteaders.

THE RAILROAD

THE RAILROAD ITSELF is one of the few things in the book I did not have to take any liberties with. The Union Pacific Railroad really did go through Columbus, just as it says in the story. The railroad crosses the Loup River at the place where Grenville Dodge originally indicated (not where Seymour tried to move it). It ran southwest across the prairie to its next stop in the town of Silver Creek, just clipping the corner of what I have designated as the Brownings' homestead claim. Silver Creek does not appear in the novel, however, because it wasn't yet built in 1863.

Believe it or not, I had selected the site for the homestead before I ever knew it was so close to the Union Pacific line. I put it there just for fun, because my brother-in-law once ran across the state of Nebraska along that same route. When I learned that the railroad was being built during those same few years after the passage of the Homestead Act of 1862, and in that very same area, I knew the story would have to have something to do with the railroad.

When I learned about Thomas Durant and his shady dealings, about Grenville Dodge and Silas Seymour, I began to think about a story in which the Brownings were somehow caught up in the midst of these intrigues. Finally, when I took a close look at where that rail line actually was, and discovered it just clips the corner of the Brownings' claim—those five acres I had Mr. Dodge agree to buy from Bram—the rest of the story came into focus.

If the railroad had crossed the Loup River a little ways farther downstream, the stretch of track from Columbus to Silver Creek would have shifted ever so slightly, and would have been about half a mile shorter than it was.

A half a mile meant big money. When the United States Congress authorized the construction of the Transcontinental Railroad, it also established the rates at which the railroad companies would be paid for building it. Across flat prairie land, that amount was $16,000 dollars for each mile of track.

It wouldn't take much for a couple of snakes like Seymour and Durant to realize that if they were to move the Loup River bridge—without informing Grenville Dodge or the U.S. Government about it—they wouldn't have to build that extra half mile of track, and could pocket the difference between the budget and the actual costs. That difference of nearly $10,000 in 1863 is roughly the same as a quarter of a million dollars today.

It would have been an easy swindle, too, except for stubborn Mr. Browning, his daughter, and her faithful prairie horse.

THE BROWNINGS

AS FOR MARIA, Klarina, Laisa, and Bram, they are wholly figments of my imagination. To the best of my knowledge, no such family actually existed, although they easily could have.

In 1848, the country of Germany went through its own civil war, in which the populace rose up against the stringent controls of Germany's aristocrats. In those days, the German people had very few guaranteed rights of any kind, and they did not like it.

Unfortunately, this uprising ultimately failed. The aristocrats—the princes and the dukes—regained control. But in the process, millions of German citizens emigrated from Germany, seeking a better life somewhere else. These people came to be known as "Forty-Eighters."

I have a personal fascination for print-ing technology and the history of print. For my own pleasure, I had it in mind that Bram should be a printer by trade, and that he should be from the German town of Mainz. Mainz is most famous for being the home of Johannes Gutenberg, who was responsible for the development of moveable type print-ing in western society.

Johannes Gutenberg

One of the grievances the German people had in their upris-ing was that they had no true freedom of the press. Bram, being a printer himself, would surely have rankled at that situation. It seemed reasonable to me that Bram and his young wife Laisa would leave Germany to come to America, one of the only na-tions at that time to have a free and independent press.

Many Forty-Eighters came to America. They established Ger-man communities in several cities, including Chicago. Printing and typesetting were skilled trades in those days, so it seemed reasonable that Bram would have been able to find work in a print shop, although he would no doubt have had to struggle to learn English quickly. I imagine that daily practice with English at his job would have helped him along.

Attitudes among immigrant families towards their native lan-guage varied. Some held tight to their heritage within the home, and spoke English only outside the home. Others fully embraced their new land, and worked hard to make English their prima-ry language. Because of Bram's need of English for his work, it made sense to me that he and Laisa would speak it even at home. Of course, no one is perfect and naturally the occasional German word or phrase sneaks through from time to time.

CLAIMS AND HOMESTEADING

IF YOU HAVE ever seen pictures of the prairie land in the midwestern states, you may have noticed that the land is divided into a patchwork of little squares. Those little squares have some big history behind them.

The Platte River and Loup River near Columbus, Nebraska

Not long after the Revolutionary War, Thomas Jefferson proposed a new method of surveying and describing land, one that better suited the needs of a growing nation than the "metes and bounds" system the Pilgrims brought from England.

The metes and bounds system only worked in places where people already lived, where landmarks such as rivers, trees, and rock outcroppings can be readily described. But it wasn't any good for land in the unsettled west, where people wanted to move but where there weren't any towns yet. To overcome this, Thomas Jefferson proposed that territories of land, such as the Northwest Territories or the Louisiana Purchase, be described on a predictable grid system.

Each such section would have two special lines, a principal meridian and a baseline. The principal meridian was whatever east-west longitude on the earth was deemed appropriate for that territory. Similarly, the baseline was an appropriate line of latitude. The point where those two lines crossed marked the origin of the survey system for that territory.

From there, the land was divided into blocks called townships, large squares six miles on each side. Townships were arranged into columns running north and south along the principal meridian. Each column was called a range, and was numbered according to how many columns east or west away from the meridian it was. Within each range, the townships were numbered in a similar fashion by how many rows they were north or south of the baseline.

Townships, being quite large squares of land, were still too big for practical use. So each township was divided into a grid of squares one mile on a side. These one-mile squares were called sections. There were thirty-six in each township, numbered in a back-and-forth pattern starting from the northeast corner. Sections were then subdivided into quarters, each containing 160 acres of land.

It is these quarter sections that were the basic unit of land claims during the westward expansion. The Homestead Act of 1862 granted settlers the right to choose any available quarter section they liked. That was a settler's claim. If the settler could live on it and work the land for five years, he could "prove up" on the claim, and the government would give him the land for good.

Holding and working a claim for five years was a hard job. Most settlers gave up and went back east, "busted." Only the toughest—or like Bram, the most stubborn—stuck it out and proved up.

Within this system, the Browning family's claim would be properly described as "The Southeast Quarter of Section 15 of Township 15 North of Range 2 West of the 6th Principal Meridian." Quite a mouthful, but it got the job done. Similarly, the land Laura Ingalls's family lived on in the Dakota Territory, during the last few books of the *Little House on the Prairie* series, is properly described as "The Northeast Quarter of Section 3 of Township 110 North of Range 56 West of the 5th Principal Meridian."

Today, the U.S. government's General Land Office has placed claim records in an online database, free for anyone to use at http://www.glorecords.blm.gov/search/. If you would like to know who came to live near the Brownings in the years after 1863, you can look up Township 15 N, Range 2 W of the 6th Principal Meridian. There are some interesting sto-ries lurking in the names and dates of the patent records you will find there.

Thomas Jefferson's system came to be known as the Public Land Survey System. Despite its wordy descriptions of sections, townships, and ranges, it proved an enormous success in managing the growing nation's land holdings. It was employed westward, starting with the Northwest Territories adjacent to the original thirteen colonies, and from there all the way to the Pacific Ocean. The grids marked out by this system have defined the United States, in patchwork squares of roads and farms, to this day.

Thomas Jefferson

About the Author

Jason Black likes to write big stories about small people. He finds inspiration for his stories in the quirky twists of history, and enjoys researching how people used to do things in days gone by. Jason lives in the Seattle area with his wife, son, and daughter, who also inspire him daily. To learn more about Jason and his books, visit him on the web at www.ElderRoad.com.